NOUMENA CONTEMPORARIES
ELEPHANTS IN OUR YARD
by M̲e̲r̲a̲l̲ K̲
Translated

When her father dies u̲n̲ _____ f
Elephants in Our Yard fi̲ _____.
As a member of a Turki̲ _____ ___g ̲i̲n̲
Switzerland, she feels unw̲ ____ ___ in her adopted homeland
and struggles to fit in and make connections with others.
Aimless and adrift, she spends a year living in a state of
uncertainty, fitfully attending lectures at the university,
taking long train rides, and returning to places from her
previous life in Prizren. Memories of her idyllic childhood
in this old Ottoman city, from which she emigrated with her
family at the age of ten, force their way into the present.

But the world of her childhood no longer exists, and she
realizes that she, too, has changed. As she tries to find a place
for herself in her new country and becomes fluent in her
adopted language, she becomes increasingly more estranged
from her mother with every new word of German she speaks.

Elephants in Our Yard is a poignant first novel about a life
marked by migration and alienation, sadness and loss, but
also by hope and new beginnings.

Praise for the German language edition

"[Kureyshi] has succeeded in using autobiographical set
pieces to write an accessible, highly topical novel that strikes
a balance between restrained language and lush, poetic
storytelling."   *Neue Zürcher Zeitung*

"Meral Kureyshi's literary treatment of her migration story
goes far beyond the description of an individual fate. In
a dense prose with strong imagery, which completely
refrains from accusatory or lachrymose tones, she cleverly
reflects on the expulsion from her childhood language and
the appropriation of her new 'mother tongue.' In this new
language, she has achieved an exceedingly remarkable feat."
Der Bund

Shortlisted for the 2015 Swiss Book Prize

ELEPHANTS IN OUR YARD
by Meral Kureyshi

Translated from the German by Robert A. Cantrick

Noumena Press
Whately, Massachusetts
www.noumenapress.com

Noumena Contemporaries are published by Noumena Press
Manufactured in the United States of America by Sheridan
Set in Palatino Linotype
Printed on acid-free paper

Originally published under the title *Elefanten im Garten*
Copyright © 2015 Limmat Verlag, Zurich

Version 1.0
ISBN-13: 9781733630115 (paperback)
Library of Congress Control Number: 2021941078

swiss arts council   The translation of this work
                      was supported by a grant from
prohelvetia   the Swiss Arts Council Pro Helvetia

Edited by R.J. Allinson
Cover design & interior layout by Rachel Thern
Cover and frontispiece photograph © jutafoto/Adobe Stock

Also available as a PDF ebook
Visit www.noumenapress.com for details

Elephants in Our Yard

Your coffin is in the ground. You wanted to be buried in Prizren. For a month I've covered my hair with a white headscarf every Friday morning and said the *Yasin*, the prayer for the dead, for you.

From the seventh-floor window I see Anne leaving the building. I know there's a Marlboro stuck between her lips. In her purse, which must be older than I am, there's at least one of those red and white cigarette packs. She's barely outside when she lights a cigarette with a lighter that she's been warming in her hand. She takes a drag on it, narrowing her eyes as though it's too bright. Her chest heaves. When she exhales, she disappears for a moment in the cloud of smoke. She doesn't like smoking alone, she never did, and now she stands there like a stove that nobody needs in summer.

Baba wanted her to quit. Anne blew smoke in his face and said a cigarette goes with a good wine, and when she stopped drinking, she said a cigarette goes with a good cup of coffee.

The purse is made of black pigskin, pigskin is cheap. It's big and has a long strap so that in winter it will go over her padded shoulder. When I search for a pair of tweezers in it, I find a little inside pocket. The zipper looks like a wound, a wound that was stitched but the thread was never removed. Tooth by tooth I open the pocket and find a wooden comb that belonged to you.

Anne takes a collapsible cane from the purse. I watch as the cane sweeps wide from left to right. Today two new canes came in the mail; the tip of the old one had worn out.

You would like our new apartment. The floors aren't carpeted, and from the seventh-floor balcony you can look out over the rooftops and see into other apartments. You always did like Bümpliz. You used to come here for shopping, a lot of your friends lived here, and you went to mosque for the Bairam prayer in the basement of a high-rise building with a large group of Albanian men.

Five years we looked for an apartment. After you died, we found one in a high-rise on the outskirts of Bern, where twenty-seven foreign and three Swiss families live.

"My, but your German is good," the landlady said to me, very loudly and distinctly.

"We've lived in Switzerland since I was ten," I replied. Ever since we moved in, we've intended to put pictures on the walls. They're still bare.

Anne goes to the school for the blind by herself. She goes shopping at Alima, the Turkish store, and takes the train to Biel to visit her friend Emine. Once a month, Franz comes to teach her new routes, which she then proudly shows off to us, leading the way while the rest of us follow. "The duck family," Maria yells from the fourth floor. She knows who in the building has had a fight, who didn't clean the washing machine after using it, who didn't remove the lint from the dryer.

My brother is twenty-two now, two years younger than I am. He wants to be a graphic artist, sleeps half the day, and his room is always dark and dirty. My sister, to whom I'm more of a mother than her own mother—my mother, our mother—is ten years younger than I am. Anne protects her as though she were a delicate piece of jewelry. She never treated us that way. When my brother was little, for a long time she beat his behind with stinging nettles when he wet the bed.

I look for more things in the wound and come across a folded piece of paper. It's the letter you sent us from Istanbul in the summer of 1991. Fifteen years have passed since then. It says you want to enter Switzerland, you ask us to follow you, to trust you. You write in capital letters.

The letter is folded into four rectangles, the paper a little brown around the folds, the writing is neat.

"A doctor's handwriting," I can hear you say. You didn't become a doctor, you cleaned doctors' offices, and when we came to visit, you put on the white lab coat that hung behind the door, we sat on the examination table, which you had covered with white paper, inhaled and exhaled deeply so that you could examine us.

When the letter arrived, Anne sat down on the sofa in our small apartment in the Kurilla quarter in Prizren and cried. My brother was sleeping on his pillow under the table. I was standing beside the open door of the house. The wind carried yellow leaves into the room. It was a warm wind, it tickled under my arms. When Anne got up and went past me over the threshold, my head turned toward her and away again. A brown eye peered from under the table. Anne's voice sounded far away.

"Baba isn't coming home."

When I licked my lips, I tasted salt.

"People are salty," Dede, my grandfather, once told me.

"Where is Baba?"

"I don't know, I don't know, I don't know!"

Anne put her head between her hands. Anne read the letter to us and wrote a letter back to Baba. Today her words slip through our fingers, and her eyes see through our words.

Anne walks as though she can see. When she stops suddenly, and I lean out the window.

"Is something wrong? Should I come down?"

She laughs, turns around, and disappears into the entry hall. Worried, I hurry to the elevator.

"You forgot to put on my makeup."

Anne "clapses" her cane, which is how she describes that action. She doesn't need it in the house. She goes into the bathroom, puts the toilet seat down, sits on it, and closes her eyes. I spread the powder on her face with my fingers, trying to cover the red patches on her cheeks. Her skin feels slightly rough.

"Open your eyes."

"How do I look? I haven't seen myself in ten years."

"You look like Fatma Girik."

She pulls the white scarf over her black locks.

I was ashamed of it. No one in our family wore a headscarf, so why did she have to wear a headscarf now, here, in Switzerland, I thought, and I told her so. Anne said I should think before I speak. That's the reason I started writing. I could write what I thought and no one told me to think first.

I was already ashamed that we couldn't buy new clothes, that we cut each other's hair, that we were the only ones who had no car or telephone, then Anne had to go and wear a headscarf, too. We had already been different before that; now we were the others.

In the kitchen Anne takes a bottle of Coke from the refrigerator. She says she could gain weight without eating, that she could double the kilos on her hips just by looking.

I think about the photos she carries in her purse. I don't have to conceal the fact that I'm going through her purse; I can do it under her eyes, which can't see me while she sips her Coke and laughs. I'm ashamed of myself.

The photos show you and Anne dancing, holding each other tight. There are lots of wine bottles on the table, and the mascara under Anne's eyes is smeared. Her lips are red. Her nails are red. In one photo you're kissing. In another one she's sitting on your lap and laughing with her head thrown back, one arm around your neck. Anne's cheeks swell. Her lips part slightly, she lets out a burp.

"That's gross, don't ever do that again."

I go to my room and slam the door behind me. I can hear her laughing.

The apartment door clicks shut. I get up right away, go back to the window. Winter is in its annual war with autumn, the battle will soon be won. I wait till she comes out of the entrance hall, lights her cigarette, and rummages in her purse for her cane. Left, right, left, right. Just before the last bend she turns and smiles broadly. She knows I'm waving to her.

Some days the first of September seems so far away that I can barely remember it—not your face, not your smell, not your hands.

Your voice, too, is gradually disappearing from my ears.

I'm afraid that someday you'll disappear completely.

From my memory, from my mouth, from my face. Aga says I look like you.

On other days it's as if you've been dead only a few days.

You lie lifeless on the bed.

No laughter in your face.

No movement in your hands.

No sight beneath your fallen eyelids.

Your jaw is tied up with my pink scarf.

Anne was standing beside Baba.

My sister sat on the chair beside him keeping her head down. Her hair covered her face. Now and then a tear dripped from the tip of her nose onto the back of her hand.

My brother tried to be strong, tried not to look me in the eye, to say nothing, tried to breathe evenly. My brother was trying to be a man.

I saw his chin tremble; mine did, too. Baba's hand was in mine. I don't know how long.

At some point it was dark; the room in the *Inselspital*, the University Island Hospital, was brightly lit. His hand had turned cold and pale. I bent and kissed it three times, bringing it first to my mouth, then to my forehead, then back again.

"I forgive you for what was on earth; please forgive me, too."

Sometimes Baba bought things on credit at the bakery in Neuenegg. I was with him once. I was behind him at the cash register as he bent forward slightly and quietly asked the cashier—whom he barely knew, who always smiled at me, whose breath smelled like cat food, who had a Serbian husband who ran the bakery, who was very nice to us—whether he could put the purchase on his tab. He said thank you with a smile, placed his hand over his heart, and inclined his head forward. I had put the bread, butter, the Nutella, a few vegetables, and the milk into the shopping bag. Baba reached for his pack of cigarettes immediately. We were hardly outside when he lit one. He blew smoke rings at the sky, I laughed. At precisely that moment—I was twelve—as he stood beside me with shining eyes, I swore I would one day have so much money that Baba and Anne would never again have to charge anything.

I swore it to the heavens between the smoke rings as loudly as I could.

Anne and I exit the Globus department store where we've been looking at nice dishes and silverware, sniffing perfumes, stroking cashmere sweaters. It's gotten cold.

Anne asks whether I have a warm sweater, I say yes, she asks what it cost. Anne asks what everything costs. She says money comes from the devil. With money you can distract people from life, lead them astray, deceive them, make them happy, kill them.

We drove into town, wandered through the stores. First Loeb's, then Voegele, later C&A, and finally EPA. Each of us was allowed to get something. I always reached for the price tag first. But I didn't want to run around in the same clothes all the time, the same shoes, so I chose violet leggings and a big T-shirt with a flower pattern. I wanted to keep them on right then and never take them off again. My brother bought candy and a wig, which he put on right away. Anne bought my sister a blond doll, and Baba got a ring for Anne—which made her finger green after a few days and lost its gold color. She never took it off. The plastic jewel fell out several times, he always glued it back in. Every month we drove into the city as soon as Baba's pay was in the bank. We all knew we couldn't spend much, but this day was the best one. We ate at McDonald's, sometimes in a pizzeria. Baba loved pizza. I watched as he cut it into real little pieces and folded the little pieces with his fork before he put them in his mouth. I tried to copy him, but I was too greedy and ate the pieces whole with my hands.

When we had money, Baba and Anne laughed a lot. When we had no money, they smoked a lot and we sat around at home. They fought, we cried in our room. My brother and I said if the light goes on right now, we'll be real rich. Or: if it starts raining right now. Or: if Baba wins the lottery.

Anne clings to my arm. When I'm with her, she doesn't need the cane. My arm gets warm where her hand is. She's wearing the ring with the green jewel that you gave her on her ring finger. The color has stopped coming off on my finger, she says, when I twist it around her finger a few times. Anne always has warm hands. She says people with warm hands get lots of love. You loved her a lot. When I say that I always have cold hands, she takes my hand in hers, warms it, and says,

"No they aren't, don't say such dumb things."

She asks me whether her hands are wrinkled. No, I say, you don't have any wrinkles, not even in your face. She smiles and knows I'm lying.

I didn't know it would be my last five minutes with Baba. He was sitting on the couch listening to music. We were talking about the apartment he wanted to go see with Anne. Next morning he complained about pains in his shoulder, so Anne wanted to postpone the appointment. Baba wanted to see the apartment no matter what. They got into the red Mercedes and drove toward Bümpliz. After five minutes Baba's heart stopped beating. Then Anne screamed.

On bath day we were all led to the cloakroom in the gym of the Brunnmatt schoolhouse in Effingerstraße. The women shared a shower room with the girls, the men shared one with the boys.

While the women and girls undressed, I fled into the hallway. Anne followed and sat beside me on the cold floor. We sat there till the others had finished showering and had left the changing cubicle.

Then we got up and went into the empty cloakroom. Anne turned her back to me and looked for something in her purse until I had undressed and wrapped a towel around my naked body. I showered quickly. When I was done, Anne, wrapped in a towel, went past me into the shower room. I got dressed, combed my hair, and packed my things in my bag. After a short time, Anne came out of the shower and I went into the bathroom. When I came back, Anne was already dressed. Freshly showered, we went back into the bunker. That was our first home in Switzerland. The green neon sign of the University Hospital Island dazzled my eyes as we crossed the dark schoolyard.

Almost every day I take the bus from Bümpliz into the city, past that air-raid shelter where we lived for two weeks. I think of you. Everything is still the same. I press my forehead against the bus window and try vainly to recognize something as we go by. I get off the bus and go down to the entrance to the bunker. The first time in fifteen years.

The iron gates are shut. I hold onto the iron gate with both hands, smell the damp walls, press my face between two ice-cold iron bars. It's dark.

Lights were on only in the apartments across the way. I watched strange people watching television. Some were standing at open windows and smoking, others were drinking tea and talking on the phone. I watched for hours, gave them names. The smoking man was Moonface; I had never seen such a round face. The woman in front of the TV was Elizabeth because she looked so much like the queen in the magazines that I flipped through at the newsstand. Her husband was Transfer. I heard this word so often that it had to be the name of a king. One evening, when Moonface called something out to me in his foreign language, it frightened me, and I ran back to the room, where all twenty-four foreigners were already asleep.

I was afraid of Moonface. He would turn us in to the security guards, they could throw our family in jail, and we'd have to spend years there. I wouldn't be able to go to school anymore. They'd give my brother to a family with no children because he was so cute.

Anne once told me that lots of married couples can't have children. She herself had toyed with the idea of giving her unborn child—which she was going to call Orhan because she liked that actor and singer so much—to Aga, my father's brother, and his wife. They couldn't have children, and my parents already had me and my brother.

The thought of giving away her child got harder for her every day. When she was seven months pregnant, she started bleeding heavily. The child's tiny legs hung from her lower body when she was sitting on the toilet. She cried loudly, held onto the child's legs with her hands, and had to be taken to the hospital. Anne lost a lot of blood and almost lost her life. The child was stillborn and was buried in a small coffin. Anne said to me later,

"I could never have given my child away. Never."

While I'm pressing my head against the cold bars, a man in military uniform comes toward me from the bunker.

14

Could I have a look inside, I ask, I'd like to see what it's like to live underground.

"There's nothing to see. It's just an air-raid shelter."

On our first day in the bunker we were led into a large room with long tables and lots of chairs where men with wet spots under their armpits were sitting. We went on, down a long hallway into a room where there were eight loft beds. Baba told us that there was only one bed available for all of us. There were seven more beds for seven more families in the same room. The gray concrete walls reminded me of our basement in Prizren.

It smelled damp and a little like vinegar. Babaanne, my grandmother, stored her hot peppers, her tomatoes, and her over-salted cheese with dill on a rickety wooden shelf.

When I had to go to the bathroom, there were already several people ahead of me. There was one toilet for the women and one for the men. A woman from Kosovo, who was also waiting, asked me in Albanian where my mother was. I understood her but couldn't answer. How can it be that people from Kosovo don't speak Albanian, she asked me.

We were part of the Turkish minority in Yugoslavia, I had to explain that to everyone. My parents could speak Turkish, Albanian, and Serbo-Croatian.

I liked listening to the strange languages in the bunker and was glad that I didn't understand them. A different melody came from each mouth.

That was the only music that there was.

There were no pictures on the walls of the bunker, no carpet on the floor, no windows with flower boxes, no Dede, and no Babaanne, either.

I was little, but big enough that I was not allowed to be little any more.

Baba wanted a red Mercedes. Traveling by train was too expensive, he said.

For five years we drove around Switzerland in a gray non-Mercedes until a policeman took away his Yugoslavian driver's license because it wasn't valid in Switzerland. Baba protested loudly; driving was the same everywhere. Baba took the first-aid course with eighteen-year-olds, the written exam, and the driver education course. Then he had to take parallel parking lessons with a driving instructor although he'd been driving for twenty years. Meanwhile, the gray non-Mercedes rusted out because it had been outside too long. Baba took it to the crusher at the scrap yard in Thörishaus, had it flattened, and, with no money, bought a red Mercedes for ten thousand francs—which he intended to pay off in monthly installments over five years.

When we went on long trips, we were not all allowed to go in the car together. Anne went by train with my brother or me or my sister.

Baba believed that if we had an accident, we shouldn't all get wiped out. Never did we all fly together to Prizren, we trickled in one by one over several days.

No one questioned it, everyone had a story about a whole family getting killed because they had traveled together. No descendants, no one left behind.

Once I asked Sarah after school how her family traveled.

Always together in the car to Italy. Always to the same house. Always in the second week of summer vacation. Sarah said that the whole family went hiking together once. One trail was so narrow that they could have gone over the edge at any time. Their father tied a rope around their waists, and they proceeded slowly in single file. He said that if anyone fell, everyone would go.

I liked that idea better, I just had to convince Baba.

When I proposed to him after school that it should be all of us or no one, he said everyone has a time to die. We can't influence it, only by suicide, and Islam forbids suicide. So we have no power over it and no idea when our time will come. I should stop thinking such thoughts because nothing good would come of it.

So, why wouldn't he travel with all of us, I wanted to know, if everyone has a time to die.

My brother and I were intolerable when we're together for long periods of time, he said. Sometimes they felt like throwing us out the window and then backing up over us till we were quiet, and because they didn't want to have to kill us, because that's forbidden by Islam, too, we were going to travel separately.

It wasn't the first or last time Baba told us the story of how he got from Venice to Switzerland.

"I tried to act as normal as possible, practiced a normal smile in the train window, ate an apple so slowly that the place where I took a bite turned brown, opened my bag and put a book in it, took it out again after a few seconds, put it on the seat beside me, adjusted my coat, tugged at my pant legs, took a drink of water. I had already refilled the bottle with fresh water at least a hundred times.

"Then it was time. I held an Italian newspaper in front of my face and tried to act nonchalant. An Albanian man in the compartment behind me had to show his papers. The customs officials questioned him, and he couldn't answer; I couldn't understand anything, either, he wasn't Italian, the officials could tell from his papers and his nose. I sipped water, put the newspaper away, picked it up again, put the book in the bag and then beside me again on the seat. It was an Italian book; I set it down open without having read any of it. The dog barked and pulled the official with him; the conductors came along behind. I had my ticket ready on the little table; I held the newspaper open.

"'Buongiorno, come stai? Che bella giornata.'

"I spoke that sentence as though I'd been doing it my whole life. I showed my ticket casually, with a flick of my wrist, more elegantly and more like an Italian even than I'd seen it done in Fellini films, with the Italian expression and gesture that I'd practiced. The conductor punched the ticket, said 'Thank you,' and wished me a pleasant journey.

"'Arrivederci, grazie,' I said after them and hoped they hadn't heard me say 'grazie.' Why should I say 'thank you' to them?

"When I looked at the newspaper in front of my face, I realized to my horror that the letters were upside down. I was so happy to get to Switzerland. I knew everything would be better in Switzerland. When I got off the train in Zurich, I kissed the ground."

In Venice I get on the train and read your diary. I find an entry on the day of my birth.

You're waiting outside the small room in your parents' house. You're waiting for me. You hear Anne scream. You want to know what I look like, you want to hold me in your arms, watch me grow up. You're nervous. You write that it's the most beautiful day of your life.

Through my eyes your writing looks as though it's under water, the letters move slightly, they blur.

I look for you in your diary, I find myself.

What would have become of us if we had stayed in Prizren? I ask myself.

I am a teacher. I have two children who are a bit spoiled and look like me. My husband works a lot, I hardly ever see him; sometimes we drive to a small house at the lake for a few days in the middle of no-where, I fall in love with my husband's best friend, with the bus driver, with the man who comes by himself to get his child from school every Monday afternoon. My husband's parents really like me, all parents like me. I want to travel, we can't afford it; the war is over, a few burned-out churches, houses, and people are remind-ers of it; my whole family lives in the same town, my best girlfriend, Gül, next door; sometimes they turn off the power four, five, six hours, to sell it to another country, there are candles all over the house. My hus-band runs a formal-wear business. We get invited to a wedding every week, I always put on a new dress from the store and put it back after the event. I am tormented by the yearning for a different life. Before the war we lived well, Anne says.

Baba is alive.

I change trains in Arth-Goldau. The train starts, I unbut-ton my coat, the train leans into the curves, I stumble over bags lying on the floor, the train leaves the station,

I look for an empty place and fall into the seat, I put my legs up on the seat opposite, my shoes on a newspaper someone left. Under my shoes I read that from now on there will no longer be a Miss Switzerland. When I tilt my foot to the side to see the last Miss Switzerland's face, the paper falls on the floor. The conductor comes, I show him my ticket wordlessly.

I put your diary in my handbag before I get off in Bern.

The first snowflakes drift through the air in the wind, like millions of fish in a great school. With every gust of wind the flakes change direction. I look at the sparkling crystals, try to focus on one, to follow it, run after it; the wind changes direction, the crystal, too, and I run after them.

You liked snow.

The sun peeks through the clouds.

I walk through the sky of white dots, run down the street after the flake; a honk, another one, I trip on the curb, the flake lands on my eyelashes. The flake begins to melt and makes my eyelid heavy, I say excuse me to the driver, who yells at me, I argue with him. I learned that from Olive Oyl, the Olive Oyl in Popeye the Sailor. My brother kept calling me Olive Oyl until he forgot my real name.

You would have been embarrassed if you had been there. You didn't like it when I yelled.

A woman in her midsixties gets into the elevator from Bern station up to the parking level with me. I'm carrying a bouquet of roses and a bag with a cake, she pushes the button, the doors close, and I say,

"That red coat looks really good on you, you're a beautiful woman."

I can't get her smile out of my head as I cross the Grosse Schanze, the park in front of the university. There is nothing to remind me of Women's Day except the Facebook photos of my cousin Alma in Prizren.

A restaurant full of well-dressed people with elaborate hairdos and a set table.

At my cousin Alma's wedding, the party was loud, hectic, and like an American movie. She played the princess, he the prince. The cake, shaped like the Eiffel Tower, was enough for all five hundred invited guests, the floor reflected the colorful shoes, twenty cameras hung from the ceiling and preserved every second of the wedding so that later each of the five hundred guests received a DVD with more than six hours of material in which they could look for themselves. The bride and groom sat on a podium the entire evening and had themselves photographed with each and every one of the guests. The preparations began two years before, the Luxory Palace had to be booked, the clothing sewn, gifts purchased. The wedding was the beginning of a life of indebtedness.

Anne phones me before I get home. You used to bring her flowers, make coffee for her, and send us ahead with cake.

"Don't you want to congratulate me? No one cares about March 8 any more."

When I arrive with flowers and cake, she cries and tells me that in Prizren this day was a big holiday. All women got flower bouquets and chocolate from their employers and jewelry from their husbands. In socialist Yugoslavia women were appreciated and honored, Anne tells me with cake in her mouth.

It's noon when I arrive at the airport in Basel. In one hour I'll fly away over Basel in an orange and white airplane. I get my book out of my backpack. Children are running around, their parents calling after them loudly, they don't want to stand at the closed departure gate for hours.

I'll begin reading my book in two weeks, on the return trip from Basel to Bern.

The passengers at the front of the line are taken aside because they have brought more than just one piece of luggage. The prominent signs cannot be missed, they say only one piece of carry-on per person and that it may not exceed 50 x 40 x 20 centimeters. A few passengers force their bags into the frame for checking the dimensions of luggage. On the airplane, a man from Ticino and his mother sit beside me. My Italian sounds as bad as his German. He tells me about his mother, her hometown, and that he was born in Switzerland. They visit his mother's family once a year in a small village that I don't know, but I pretend to know where it is and forget its name as soon as the man from Ticino puts the headphones over his ears to end the stressful conversation. Two girls, whose ages I guess at seven, kick the back of my seat so hard that it shakes me. I close my eyes and take a deep breath.

The sun burns on my skin as I get off the plane. Two buses bring all the passengers the few meters to the gate of the new airport in Pristina, where Ismail is waiting for me. I arrive an hour late. When we embrace, our upper bodies collide so hard it knocks the wind out of me briefly. For a moment we're children again, no time has passed, no war has devastated the country, no farewell has separated us. We get into the burning-hot old Volvo that Ismail's brother bought for 150 euros. He is unemployed. All the windows are open, we drive, we sing the Turkish songs playing on the radio, I stick my head out the window. My body is heavy as the heat.

In Mustafa's store I bought sweet powder in every possible flavor and color to mix into syrup. I ate the powder right out of the bag before I went home to help Anne pack our last items.

I sat beside Anne as she carried my brother in her arms and cried. Aga drove us to the airport. Kneeling on the back seat I looked out the back window. The clouds were reflected in a wet spot on the ground.

"May your journey go like water, light and carefree. Flow, discover, just do not forget. Come back soon, as lightly as you flowed away," were Dede's last words as I hugged him. Babaanne stood by smiling with an empty tin pail in her hands.

We drove through the narrow streets, past the people, past the houses, the mosques, the old hammam, the post office, beneath the power lines, through the city. I looked out the window. My brother clung to Anne with both arms. I didn't want Anne to see my face, so I pressed my forehead and nose against the window glass. Distorted images of the men drinking tea were reflected on the door handle. The city went by and remained unchanged in our memories for thirteen years.

It smells sweet as I walk past the grocery store. I have no desire to go in. Spring is creeping out of the moist earth, stretching, awakening the trees and the colors. A small park is hidden among the old houses, which are painted white. Dilapidated and renovated houses stand close beside each other. Some collapsed years ago or burned down.

Most properties have stayed the same, still have tall metal gates through which you pass to get into a courtyard. Every yard hides behind walls. In Prizren, people hide their beauty, all that they own, which they are afraid of losing. Envy curses and destroys, I hear you say. That's why every house is decorated with a blue eye that is supposed to protect it from the evil eye.

Superstition is forbidden in Islam, so people call it tradition. Every day I take with me a fresh blue *mendil*, an embroidered handkerchief; I lost my blue eye before you died.

I cut my hair, I watch it fall to the floor, one tuft at a time. I sever every single memory from my head with the big fabric shears. They carry a burden on their tips till they turn into long forks that stab me in the back.

"You won't turn your soft hands into rough stones with scouring powder, no one will be able to hear where you come from, no one will be able to see your past."

Your voice sounded as though you were reading out loud from a book. You looked at the floor and took a long drag on your cigarette. Half of it turned to ash and fell onto the table where it lay until you smeared it with your hand.

People say "*mashallah*" three times loudly and in my face when they compliment me. A little spit always comes with it. This, too, protects against evil and envious looks, they say. During the conversation I cannot wipe the spit away, out of courtesy.

"How are you, your mother, your sister, your brother?"

"What is your sister doing, your brother, your mother?"

I hope the conversation will end soon.

"Please relay our warmest greetings to your mother, your sister, your brother."

I feel the droplet of spit distinctly, it eats into my skin.

"I am supposed to bring you fondest greetings from Hatice, Fatma, Raside, Emran, Sengül, and Ceylan."

My hand twitches, grips the mendil tightly.

"I almost forgot, warmest greetings from my daughter, Gülay."

Who is this woman, anyway, who keeps spitting in my face, and who are these people from whom she brings me greetings?

"Goodbye, Aunt." Thank God you can address all older women that way. "I hope we see each other again soon."

"Yes, come visit me sometime."

Shortly after she turns away from me I rub my face almost raw with the mendil, which has become quite warm in the palm of my hand.

After a few days, no evil eye can curse me, my face has become so polluted from all this mashallah blowing.

Suddenly everyone is upset. They say I'm a woman, I should groom myself, I look terrible, I'm no longer in puberty, I'm twenty-four now, I should go to the dermatologist, at the very least I should wear makeup. Before I cut my hair off, everyone said I should cut my hair because I looked like a gypsy, now it's short, now they say I look like a little child, I had such beautiful long hair.

Sometimes I visit you. Your soul was assigned to your body for forty-six years. For half that time you were my father.

You lie beside Dede, your aunt, and your grandfather, on your back, naked, shrouded in a long, white linen cloth.

My brother bought seven meters of it at the Loeb department store in Bern.

Babaanne insisted on being buried a few meters north of Dede. She wanted to lie beside her mother; she revered her mother, wanted to name me after her.

Two months before I came into the world in the little room in my grandparents' house, my parents drove to Belgrade. Anne wanted to go to the zoo. After five minutes she paused for a long time at the deer enclosure, Baba could not budge her from it. She shared the nuts she had bought with the animals, he walked around the zoo by himself. When he came to get her to go home, she cried. She said one of the deer stared at her stomach. He pleaded with her to come along because people were staring at her.

When I was a few months old, an old woman came to visit and said to Anne that my name had an Arabic origin and meant "deer princess." Anne cried out that she knew it, that the deer had wanted to tell her something.

Baba laughed, and the old woman said,

"Kismet," it's just fate.

My parents had given me any old name to avoid having to call me Ferdane. Ferdane, that was my great grandmother's name. Anne yelled at Baba after I was born, "Ferdane? Never. What an ugly old name, no way will I give my daughter that name." Aga came into the room and said softly,

"I have a name."

"Ok, ok, anything, just not Ferdane. Go tell that to your mother."

Babaanne was a domineering and very pretty woman, whom nobody wanted to contradict. My dear and very quiet Dede loved her too much to try to talk her out of anything.

"You got your stubborn head from her and your gentle heart from Dede," you told me before you disappeared forever.

Almost every day I entered my grandparents' courtyard though a big gate with iron bars. I walked through the flower-covered yard, over the paving stones. Dede grew up in this two-story house. It smelled of tomatoes, peppers, and onions, cucumbers climbed the white-painted wall. Before the front door stood a large shoe cabinet where I put my shoes beside Dede's Friday shoes. A long hose lay coiled on the ground, which Dede used to water the flowers, vegetables, fruit, and trees in the yard. I stood on the carpet in my socks in front of the wooden doorway, opened it, poked my head into the house. The walls were painted pale green and hung with a mirror and lots of pictures.

Babaanne was sitting in the kitchen–living room on the patterned carpet with her head bent forward. She was rolling her long hair into a coil on the back of her head with both hands and stuck a needle through it. She put a small, white bowl of *kina*—henna—on her lap, stuck her finger into it halfway, and let it soak for a while. After that, she couldn't touch anything for a few hours, until the kina was dry. Then her fingers were orange brown. She did that once a week.

I come to a large gate. With great effort I push it open and walk across the yard along an asphalt path. The house is right beside me, some of the tiles on the roof are broken, white plaster lies in shards on the ground, the windows and doors are shut. "The little witch's house," you always called it.

I go to the big house opposite it and give two short rings. I recognize her voice immediately. Fatma yells from the balcony,

"Who's there? What do you want?"

"You don't recognize me?"

"Oh my goodness, you're the little one. Come, come in, no I'll come down, just a moment, do you want something to drink? Can I offer you something to eat?"

I look up, grab the back of my neck and squeeze it a little, it's gotten stiff.

I hear her steps, hear her clumping hastily down the stairs.

She stands in front of me in her bathrobe. Over her shoulder I can see into the house. She hugs me, smells of raspberry jam and sweat.

"Let's have a look at you, you've become a woman. I can't believe it. Who came with you? Your Anne and your Baba came to visit me a few years ago, I was so happy to see them again."

I ask about Mrki. She brings me to him.

"Mrki has become an old man."

He's not as black as he was before. He snuffles my hand briefly, tries to recognize me through his long eyelashes.

My brother and I played with Mrki every day. He ran after us, and we ran away screaming. When we stumbled, he jumped on us and played man and wife with us, as we called it. I ran into the house and shut myself in. When Anne asked why I had locked myself in, I said Mrki had bitten me. Then he was put into his dog house for a few hours and chained up. That did not make me feel sorry at all. Fatma was watching once when Mrki tried to play that game with me. She started laughing and said he was doing that to me because he thought I was a girl poodle with my dark locks hanging over my ears.

"Can I go into the house?" I ask Fatma.

We lived in this house before we emigrated to Switzerland.

"After the war, an Albanian woman rang my doorbell," she said. "She had neither children nor a husband to take care of her. She asked me if I had anything to eat, since she had not eaten in days, and a place where she could sleep. She had been driven out of her village and had lost everything. I felt sorry for the poor thing. I gave her food and let her live in the little house. My husband is dead, my children have moved out, with her I had a bit of company. That was ten years ago."

Fatma knocks on the door softly and goes into the house. A small woman with short, dark hair greets me cordially. She talks to me, I do not understand a word. Fatma explains to her why we have showed up so suddenly and that I don't speak Albanian. After that she only smiles. She grins uninterruptedly with rotten teeth in her mouth, making me a little uncomfortable.

The floor is covered by a light-brown floral rug, the paint on the walls is peeling off, the windows have not been cleaned in a long time. The kitchen–living room was bigger in my memory. Fatma says of course the old house needs to be renovated, that everything is gradually deteriorating since no one is around anymore who could do it.

"I'm older, too, and as long as she's still here, I'm not collecting any rent, so I don't have the money for it."

We go into the other room, which is used as a storage room. Fifteen years ago there was a round table with four chairs in the middle of the room, two leather sofas against the wall, and opposite them a small TV. Where once a lamp hung from the ceiling only a hole remains. On the veranda there was a low couch with a small table in front of it. Now the gray floor is strewn with trash. I go down the stairs and look at the house from the yard. The quince tree partially obscures my view.

Once Anne cut her hand when I wanted to eat a quince. She was bleeding so much that three towels were drenched with her bright blood. It was my fault, because she had said that I would be late for school if I didn't get going, but I had insisted on the half of a quince.

A woman stoops to come into the yard through a small door in the wall of the neighboring house, she comes toward me. She's carrying a broom, embraces me and kisses me.

"Mashallah, you look the same as ever, I recognized you right away. Do you remember who I am?"

"No."

I wipe my sleeve over my spit-covered face.

"You always came through this little door into our courtyard on the other side and played for hours with my daughter, Gül, who is four and a half months younger than you. You liked her a lot and hid from your mother when she came looking for you. You always disappeared. It's so nice to see you. Tell me, how is it in Switzerland? It must be so beautiful there. I have a friend in Basel who brings me Toblerone every summer. Even though we can get Toblerone here, around the corner in Mustafa's store, it's something different. It tastes different, much better."

The streets are narrow and crooked, and it's as if the many power lines hold the whole city together. I try to walk between the cars, cars are parked everywhere, on the sidewalk, in front of the houses, on the street, in front of the stores, the mosques. Many with German or Swiss license plates. Suddenly I'm standing in front of a pink building. I recognize the smell immediately, wood and a bit of Javelle water and a little bit of paint. The large portrait of Tito no longer hangs on the wall.

Every morning, all the pupils gathered in this entrance hall and sang Turkish songs. Now I'm standing in the middle of it all alone. Beside the entry gate there are three large placards with photos of pupils and their names stuck on them, neatly divided by nationality. On the first placard there are fifteen Turkish pupils, on the second one twenty-six Serbian, and on the third sixty-eight Albanian. Before the war, this was a Turkish school.

It's spring vacation, no one except the caretaker is there. He's sitting in a little room biting into a sandwich and watching a soccer game on a TV that's as big as the palm of my hand. I go up the stairs to the second, the third, the fourth, the fifth floor, walk down the empty corridors, enter a classroom, and sit down at a desk. The room smells of pencils, new notebooks, and old books. The desk is scratched. "*Gökhan ve Sibel*" is carved in the middle of the desk inside a heart.

I write my name on the blackboard with chalk then smudge the letters with the palm of my hand until you can't read them anymore.

Back in Bümpliz, I stay in bed all day, I don't change, I don't brush my teeth, I don't talk to friends, I don't phone Anne, I have no desire to read nor even to think. I fall asleep again and again, when I wake up, I feel heavy, I'm hungry. I read your diary. The wind blows the rain onto my desk, which is in front of the window. The drops fall on the wood. When the telephone rings, I don't take the call, when I do, I argue with the person who asks how I'm doing. On days like this I tell myself everything is a dream, that I live in an illusion without realizing it. Something terrible is going to happen again.

I sit on the floor, leaning against the wall. The sun shines on the top of the mirabelle tree that I can see through my window.

"Do you see where you are?"

Baba picked me up and set me on the high wall so that I could climb down on the other side. My brother came over with me, giggling the whole time and imitating Bruce Lee's stances, which he saw on TV with Baba.

Whenever there was a rerun at night, Baba came into our room and woke up my brother, so quietly that I could hear it. They snuck out together, sat in front of the TV and put on headphones and laughed out loud. After a while, Anne came out of their room, yelled at them, and turned off the TV. My brother crawled back into bed, Anne kept on yelling.

"Goddamned ass, you son of an ass. Why in the hell are you handing me plastic flowers? Stop laughing right now," Anne yelled at Baba.

"When someone throws stones at you, give him bread," Baba said.

I heard the door slam, open again, and close again softly.

"Come on, you ass, or someone will see us, hurry up," I said to my brother.

We changed and kept jumping into the water until we were almost collapsing from hunger, then we strolled out through the exit of the swimming pool, whose adjoining entrance we had never used. Anne and Baba were waiting for us with food on a blanket under a mirabelle tree.

A little girl in school uniform with her hair carefully tied back. The pink bow is hidden in her locks. She sits, unmoving, at a desk in the classroom. Only her eyes move, looking nervously from left to right. As though someone were showing her two pictures, an original and a copy, on which she is supposed to find the differences. Her eyes drift back and forth, her head does not move, until a deep male voice asks,

"What is your name, kizim?"

The girl introduces herself and explains what she has brought in the school bag lying beside her on the table. She takes everything out and tells long and complicated stories. At the end, she recites a poem and smiles shyly. Her voice sounds strange.

Baba smiled at me when I told him about this TV program about the "Slobodan Surcevic" school and said,

"You did that very well, and how loudly and confidently you recited your poem. I am proud of you. You're a little star."

His index finger pointed out the window at the sky above. We had been in Prevalac for two weeks on a ski vacation, in the Serbian mountains. Celebrated my seventh birthday there. It was very warm in the hotel room.

The first night, after Anne and my brother were already in bed, I lay on the sofa pretending to be asleep. Baba was standing at the open window in his white T-shirt, smoking a cigarette. I watched him out of one eye, trying to keep the other one closed. What was he looking at? I admired him, the way he could just stand there for so long. I could hear his breath.

He breathed in and out loudly and evenly. Sometimes when he exhaled a little smoke came out of his nose.

I tried to breathe with him, also only through my nose. I couldn't, I thought that was because I had only one eye open. It took so much effort to keep the one eye shut that I couldn't breathe evenly. I opened my mouth wide and took a deep breath.

Baba closed the window and I my open eye. He wasn't supposed to see that I was awake. I could hear his breath become louder with each step. He picked me up, and I smelled the cigarette. He carried me to bed carefully then quietly closed the door behind him. When he was gone, I got out of bed, waited till he was in his room and had turned off the light, then I tiptoed down the dark corridor and stood by the window where Baba had stood. It was dark out.

I open my eyes, get out of my bed, and go to the door. When I open it, you're standing there. I look at you and move slowly in your direction. You look at me, come closer, embrace me.

"I'm visiting you," you say softly in my ear. "I cannot come often, only once every two weeks."

"Tell me what it's like there and how you are!"

"I'm well. So where is the video camera?" you ask, and search the whole house for it.

"Where is it? I want to prove to all of you that I'm really here with you. We have to capture this moment."

I'm happy to see you.

The first snow, the pictures on the wall, the pigeons on the wet streets, and, of course, us. The camera was your constant companion. The embarrassing school programs, my first attempts to put on makeup, the fights between me and my brother. The video camera was always there, and now you can't find it. You've never forgotten where you left it.

"When will you come again?" I ask.

"I don't know, dear, but I'm here now!"

You hug me again and press your cheek against mine. Your beard tickles me, and I open my eyes.

"Where are the vacuum-cleaner bags? Where are they? You never remember where you put things. Do I have to take care of everything in this house?" Baba yelled.

Anne looked in the kitchen cabinets, under the sofa, behind the curtains.

I looked in my clothes closet, which I could no longer close, so great was the disorder in it. Under my bed I reached for a rolled-up, dusty poster with Leonardo DiCaprio on it. I kissed his mouth and closed my eyes. My first kiss was with Leonardo; until then, no boy had ever kissed me. Only on New Year's Eve, once in the housing for asylum seekers in Wilderswil, when I was ten. People I didn't know hugged me and wished me a happy new year. A man from Sri Lanka came up to me. When he was standing in front of me, he smiled at me, and I could smell his sweat. He gripped my arms tightly, bent down to me and stuck his tongue in my mouth. My eyes flew wide open, and I saw him in front of me, blurry. Then I lashed out wildly, tore myself away, and ran outside. Behind the house, I had to throw up again and again till I was empty. Then I washed my tongue with snow until I was bleeding from my mouth.

There was not a second in my life when I was not in love with someone. I cried for days, held photos in my hands and sobbed to Mariah Carey or Whitney Houston. Sometimes I turned the music up real loud, stood in front of the mirror, and watched myself cry. For years I was secretly in love with Florian. Every day I saw him with other girls in the schoolyard. Even though we were in the same class, he didn't notice me. One Thursday I summoned all of my courage and wrote him a letter.

"Did you find them?" Baba yelled outside the door to my room. I hid Leonardo under my blanket and shook my head, which he could see only from behind.

"Is the back of my head flat?"

"No, the back of your head is pretty."

"I didn't ask if it's pretty, I want to know if the back of my head is flat, because when I was a baby you wrapped me up like a mummy, and I had to lie on my back for months."

"The back of your head definitely is not flat because we wrapped you up. Who told you that nonsense?"

"So the back of my head *is* flat. I knew it, and you just confirmed it. Thanks. I can't do anything about it, you know. You don't have to look at it if you don't like it.

Baba shook his head and left the room.

My brother looked in the bathroom, under the woven rug, which was always a little damp. He rummaged through the dirty clothes in the laundry basket.

"You have blood in your underpants."

He held the underpants tightly between his index finger and thumb, away from himself, and ran through the whole house with me after him.

"Give it to me, you idiot!" I yelled and tore the panties away from him, then Baba reappeared in the room.

In the bathroom I ran cold water in the basin. Cold water dissolves blood, Anne said once.

The first time I bled I was ashamed of it. I was having sharp pains and couldn't tell Anne the reason until she figured it out for herself.

"You're a woman now. When I became a woman, I celebrated with my grandmother. We had sweets in coffee houses, drank tea, bought new clothes, and she gave me a bracelet and gold chain."

I didn't want any celebration, any gold, and I didn't want sweets at all. I was in pain.

Naturally I said nothing to Baba. I was just sick once a month. That was good enough for him, and he didn't ask anything more about it, which I found very soothing.

I didn't want to be a woman.

"Go make me a coffee, my nerves are shot. You're all driving me crazy."

Anne disappeared into the kitchen without a word, I rushed into the living room, stood with my back to the TV so that Baba couldn't see anything.

"Can't you make your own stupid coffee? You're not a baby. How many times do I have to tell you not to leave your socks lying in the living room beside the sofa? Do you have to get on my nerves every day? And the next time you ask Anne to do something, say 'please'! She's not your employee, so don't you ever yell at her again, understand?"

I ran out of the apartment, slamming the doors, went up the stairs to the big terrace, locked myself out, and stayed there until the sun got tired. No one came up to check on me. After a while I was cold and got hungry. I went back into the apartment reluctantly to get a roll. Anne was lying on the sofa on her back; Baba lay on his right side on his arm, his back to me. He had put his left leg on Anne's thighs and his left arm on her stomach. His head was on her breast, and she had her left arm around him, she was holding the back of her right hand over her eyes. They were asleep. I stood beside them for a long time, then I looked for the camera, in the kitchen cupboards, behind the radiator, under the TV table. I found it in a handbag and took a picture of them together. I put the camera in the drawer of my desk with my diary.

The color film would never get developed.

The sun dazzles me as I come out of the main university building. I sit down on the railing of the terrace and watch the cars parking below. The cell phone in my bag rings.

Anne tells me about the new friend with whom she took a long walk, and I tell her about Kleist's *Käthchen*. Am I already on the train to Zurich? Anne asks. I jump up, startled, when I hear the electronic female voice.

"It's one fifty-eight p.m."

Anne wears a talking watch that is so loud I can hear its female voice. The cell phone glows through my fabric handbag as I run for the train. I notice that I haven't ended the call, I hear Anne's loud voice from the handbag.

When I reach the platform, out of breath, the train to Zurich has already left. At the departure schedule board I take a deep breath, unbutton my jacket, and reach into my handbag. Anne has already hung up.

"Can you tell me when the next train to Wilderswil leaves? I forgot my glasses at home."

"In exactly five minutes."

A short woman in hiking shoes and rain jacket. She smiles at me, asks where my trip is taking me. She has discovered traveling only recently. Previously she hardly ever went away, she had to cook for a husband, take care of the children.

"Now that Ernst is in heaven, I can do what I want."

"To Wilderswil, I'm going to Wilderswil, too," my voice says to her.

With our few belongings distributed between two suitcases, Anne carrying one and Baba the other, we crossed the street. The air smelled like earthworms. Baba was smoking. He didn't say a word while we waited for the train in Bern.

My brother and I were excited, we were running around, shouting and fighting.

"Cut it out. Sit down here. I don't want to hear another peep out of you until the train gets here. Do you understand me?"

The people around us were shaking their heads. After that my brother and I were as quiet as snow.

Since our arrival in Bern, two weeks earlier, we had watched the departing trains from the university terrace every day.

We were going to study there one day, in this old building, Baba said.

We leaned out the open window of the train. My hair wrapped around my face.

"That would be a nice house for us, with a trampoline."

"No, that one over there with the pretty flowers in the yard."

The feeling of being almost unable to breathe and the speed, which nearly tore me out the window, were so exciting I couldn't stop doing it. The wind was loud, we shouted at each other. Anne kept tugging at our clothing, yelling that we should sit down immediately, but we didn't. Baba laughed, he would have loved to stick his head out the window if Anne hadn't stopped him with dirty looks.

We all marveled at how soft and comfortable the seats were. It was completely quiet when I sat down again. Well-dressed people, hiding their faces behind big newspapers. Baba took a plastic knife out of the bag, broke open a roll with his big hands, spread soft cheese on it, and put turkey ham on it. Soon, the floor was covered with bread crumbs, and chocolate was stuck to the table. Anne rubbed the chocolate off my cheek with a handkerchief and a little spit. I screwed up my face so much that it must have frightened the conductor, who suddenly appeared. He looked at our tickets, which Baba pulled out of his vest pocket.

"This is first class, you have to move to second class."

He pointed the way for us several times with his finger.

The train ride takes an eternity. Annemarie, that's the name of the woman in hiking shoes, sits down beside me.

"Provisions," she says loudly. Would I like an apple? They're from her garden, she stores them in her cellar.

I would much rather open the window and stick my head out.

"Much too dangerous."

"What did you say? I didn't understand you." She was staring at my mouth.

"I said it was much too dangerous when you could still open the windows on trains."

"Right, you said it. It was much too dangerous, all those children hanging out the windows."

The mountains come closer, single-family houses with children jumping on trampolines in the front yard. Villages that never see the sun fly past me.

"Have you ever been to Wilderswil?"

"Yes, I lived here a long time ago, but I don't remember it very well."

I didn't like the old hotel, I had expected it to be different and wanted to go back, not to the bunker but to one of the nice houses overgrown with ivy in the Schlösslistraße by the Inselspital.

Wilderswil was the name of the village at the bottom of the mountain near Interlaken.

43

This village was creepy. Baba showed a man a piece of paper with the address, then we followed him across a wide street running between traditional wooden houses. A woman came up to us, spoke briefly with Baba and Anne, then we went into the former hotel. Inside, the walls were made of dark wood, there were lots of tables and chairs in the room, like in a restaurant. I was looking forward to our vacation, because Baba said it would be a very nice vacation. Behind the counter was a group of men from Sri Lanka.

It said "Recreation Room" on one of the doors, I read it aloud but didn't understand anything. My brother repeated it all day. It was a large room, a TV was attached to the ceiling, a few children sat in front of it watching Pinocchio. My brother sat down with them and stared at the box. Pinocchio's nose grew and grew through the whole classroom, all the way to the blackboard. My brother grabbed his nose. I followed Anne and Baba up the stairs to the second floor. A long, red carpet ran down the hallway, left and right were lots of doors with numbers. We stopped at door number twenty-two. That was the second place we lived in Switzerland. Before we were sent to Neuenegg.

In Interlaken Annemarie and I transfer to a regional train. She clings to my arm, talks about her children, whom she has not seen for a long time. Her granddaughter looks like me, she says. I reach into my handbag, after rummaging for a long time I pull out a chocolate bar.

"They all live so far away, I'd like to have them with me, and I'd like to visit them more often. But they have so much to do, they don't always have time to come to Bern. I understand it well."

"Would you like some chocolate? Warms the hands, my mother says."

She eats one row, I hand her another.

Soon the train arrives in Wilderswil, and I toss the package into the wastebasket under the little table between me and Annemarie, on which *"Iyi Yoculuklar"* is misspelled.

"Iyi Yolculuklar" would be right, "Have a Good Trip." I get out and wrap the pink scarf around my neck twice.

"I was very happy to meet you, perhaps we'll meet again."

I sit down on a bench in the railroad station and call Anne.

"Do you remember where the immigrant shelter was?"

"This village is in the southern part of Bödeli. Wilderswil is a starting point for trips into the Jungfrau region or into the Bernese Highlands in general. Wilderswil has sixteen hotels, motels, and inns with nine hundred beds and vacation apartments. Swimming and water sports are available in the nearby lakes Thun and Brienz. There are hiking trails and the railroad discovery route, 'See Nature From the Train,' which runs along the Lütschine River to the village of Zweilütschinen."

It says on the sign beside me.

Every Friday our family got twenty-one francs. Baba asked the woman who was in charge of our case why he was not allowed to look for a job, that was not enough money. With the F ID card no one would hire him. Baba would be liable to prosecution. He slammed his fist against the wall, then he smoked a cigarette with his bloodied hand.

Baba had let his hair and beard grow. Anne no longer paid any attention to how she dressed, she no longer went to the hairdresser, and the red no longer covered her fingernails completely.

"Anne, please, can't you make an effort? It can't be that hard. Tell me how I get to this stupid hotel, come on, just tell me."

45

I search for the home on my cell phone and get the web page of the immigration service of the canton of Bern.

"Asylum seekers are persons who have filed an application for asylum in Switzerland and are in the asylum application process. During the application process they have the fundamental right to remain in Switzerland. In general, foreigner IDs may be issued to asylum seekers for a period of not more than six months but in no case past the date set for leaving the country."

That asylum application process took thirteen years in our case.

Thirteen years not allowed to leave Switzerland.

Thirteen years without legal work.

Thirteen years in fear of being deported.

After thirteen years I had become a woman and my grandparents were dead.

"Provisional admission may be granted to persons whose application for asylum has been denied but who nevertheless cannot return to their homeland, especially if it is in a state of war, which would render deportation inappropriate or materially impossible. The F ID card is issued for twelve months and must be renewed annually. In fact, almost no holders of an F identity card leave Switzerland, for example Somalis living in Switzerland since 1992 or those who immigrated from the former Yugoslavia between 1993 and 1995."

"Tschüss, bye, I love you Anne, you who carried me under your heart for nine months and gave birth to me with unimaginable pain."

Anne likes to talk about my birth, above all when she wants to give me a bad conscience.

"Yes, Anne, I'm sorry, yes, I promise I'll never yell at you again."

"Hadi tschüss. Tschüss de."

"Tschüss, Tschüss."

Surely I'll be able to remember something.

"During the initial period after submittal of application for asylum, the person seeking asylum is not permitted to engage in gainful employment. Accordingly, alien IDs will bear the notation 'gainful employment prohibited.'

After the first three months, the alien ID will be renewed with the notation 'Without gainful employment.'"

At the bus stop there are young people in ski outfits, others carry sleds on their shoulders. It's spring vacation.

A soldier in uniform is waiting for the bus that goes through the village. Every fifteen minutes, up the main street and back down again.

On the insignia sewn onto his upper arm it says "SWISSCOY KFOR," I see the Kosovo coat of arms and under it the Swiss one. I step closer. When he turns around and takes a step back, I brush the hair out of my face, he looks at me, and I say,

"Are you flying to Pristina?"

What a dumb question, I think.

"No, not yet."

"Oh, ok."

"Yes."

"Have you ever been to Prizren?"

"Yes, I'm stationed there."

"You know what? My family and I come from Prizren. We lived in this village for a while when we came to Switzerland. Did you grow up here?"

"Yes, exactly."

"What a coincidence."

47

"Yes, exactly."

Then he turns away from me before I can go on.

I tear bits of skin off with my fingernails until there's blood on my fingers.

Blood tastes like my earring.

Once your lip bleeds, it keeps bleeding until you forget what blood tastes like.

I don't find the hotel and return to Bern.

"Tickets, please."

Three men in orthopedic shoes with their pant legs turned up, black jackets, and the unmistakable bulge of belt pouches. They get up at the same time and go through the number twelve bus, and everyone shows them their tickets, smiles at the men, wishes them a nice day. The happy trio does not stay long in the bus, because everyone has a ticket. I do too. The disguised man, who does not want to be recognized as a fare inspector but can be recognized a hundred yards away, does not check my ticket carefully. He trusts me, and I travel through the Old Town of Bern, past the bank of the Lombards, who once upon a time came from northern Italy and in the middle of the thirteenth century opened the first bank in Kramgasse on the spot where two years ago the used bookstore Hegnauer was. It's Saturday morning, market morning in Münstergasse.

When I get home and am about to take off my shoes, the doorbell rings. I ask through the intercom who it is. A man speaks in French, and I go down.

The anxiety rose into my head. I felt warm and sick. As soon as anyone entered the compartment where we were sitting my heart throbbed so hard I thought I could see it through my sweater. We had to travel only three stations with the regional train, from Neuenegg to Flamatt. My brother was relaxed, looked out the open window and laughed at the sheep, which were making such funny noises, as if they were making fun of us. He poked me and wanted me to look. I kept my eyes on the doors.

Two men entered the compartment. I saw through the disguise immediately. That calm way of looking out the window, the slow movements. The orthopedic shoes, the black jackets with the bulge.

"Tickets, please."

My entire body was covered in goose bumps. The men transfixed me with their eyes, I couldn't move. My brother was still laughing and didn't notice them. One of them repeated the sentence,

"Tickets, please."

"Our tickets flew out the window, I just had them in my hand, and when I sat down, they were gone."

The men kept smiling, let my brother keep talking till he stared at me questioningly and didn't know what to do. But I was speechless.

The men exchanged glances with a twinkle in their eyes and made us fill out a slip of paper with all our personal information. I was Sarah Krebs, lived at Eseligasse two, and my phone number was that of the telephone booth at the Neuenegg station, where we made phone calls every day.

The doorbell rings. When I get downstairs, a man wearing makeup and no jacket is waiting there, shivering, and as soon as I open the door, he starts talking to me.

He must get back to Paris, he has no money, he doesn't know where he's going to sleep, he's hungry, he says, there are no sympathetic people in Switzerland, he talks loudly, more loudly, he falls silent.

I offer him food, a warm sweater, my help in finding a place to stay, to pay part of his ticket, which I'll go help him purchase.

He yells at me, he wants money, he says I'm a spoiled, rich brat who is well off, who always had it good, has never had problems, that I'm greedy.

He goes and leaves me standing in the entryway beside the mailboxes.

A Frigider, used, it's true, but like new, hardly any damage, just one small, barely visible scratch on its red surface, and it was big and cost hardly anything, stood in the kitchen in Neuenegg beside the round kitchen table covered with a white tablecloth.

This red Frigider made more noise at night than the little gray one we'd had before, that I liked, that they'd put in the scrapyard beside hundreds of cars. Our old red car had already been put in the scrapyard, where the crusher with its sixteen giant hammers, that weighed more than twenty tons, had pressed it into a plate and laid it on a tower of other plates. Rats, worms, and insects lived in those plate structures with their families. With our plate another used but like-new apartment became available, with just one small, hardly noticeable scratch on its red surface.

Hundreds of new apartments were built every day.

Anne no longer had to put meter-long cloths under the new Frigider overnight, which by morning had soaked up all the water and smelled like jeans in the rain.

In this Frigider nothing melted. Nothing froze, either.

"How practical," said Anne.

"How American," said my brother.

"How big," said Baba.

"Frigider," said my sister.

Sarah turned twelve on February 5th.

My savings were enough for a red candle shaped like an angel, three sticks of incense, and a black-and-white poster of an Indian chief. I wrapped them all up in used gift-wrapping.

I was surprised that Sarah didn't come to school that morning and decided to surprise her at home at noon. Sarah lived with her family at the edge of the woods in a big house with a yard, up the hill from the school in Neuenegg. Sarah's mother opened the door.

"Hello, I haven't seen you in a long time. How are you?"

"I'm fine, is Sarah home?"

She turned her head and called to her. I stared at the back of her neck and her short blond hair. Her neck was as thin as my upper arm. You could hardly see her breasts. When Sarah came to the door, she laughed. She didn't look especially sick.

"Happy birthday." I reached into my bag with both hands and pulled out the little package.

"Thanks. You shouldn't have."

Sarah was as friendly as ever.

Between her arm and the door frame I could see into the living room. Simone, her cousin, was there, a few of her friends, her whole family, and still others, whom I didn't know. On the table there were a lot of colorful packages. On the other table I could make out a big cake. Her mother came back to the door and saw my package, smiled, and thanked me. She said I shouldn't have, and held Sarah firmly by the shoulder.

"Come along, now, they're all waiting for you."

Sarah thanked me again, too, and held out her hand.

"Wouldn't you like to come in?" I heard softly, as the door was closing.

"No, no, I don't have time, I have to go home. See you tomorrow at school."

On the way home I took a long walk through the woods and sat down under a birch tree. I watched the snow fall from the leafless branches.

Sarah, that's what I wanted to be called. I hated my name, which no one could remember. When strangers asked me my name, I always said, "Sarah."

If our paths had not crossed at school, we definitely would not have become friends. At recess on the first day of school I fell off the jungle gym. For a moment I couldn't breathe or even move. Sarah was the only one who came running up to me, asked me something, which I didn't understand. "Sarah," she pressed her index finger to her chest and said, "Sarah." I had to laugh, the situation reminded me of the scene when Jane tells Tarzan her name.

After school we didn't have much contact, but we kept running into each other. She went to concerts by Gotthard, DJ Bobo, and Florian Ast; I listened to Tupac, Snoop Dogg, and Jay-Z. For my thirteenth birthday she gave me a big surprise. I didn't have a clue. Her mother drove us to Zurich, and I saw the big poster: "DJ Bobo, live in Zurich."

The hall was already half-filled with screaming, shoving people. I watched Sarah as she pushed into the crowd and kept turning around to me, beaming across her whole face and towing me along by the hand. Her shoulder-length blond hair covered her neck.

"It's about to start!" Sarah yelled in my direction and brushed the bangs out of her eyes.

A man standing beside me lifted me up onto his shoulders in happy anticipation of the DJ Bobo concert. He hopped through the crowd with me. I held so tight to his hair that he cried out in pain. Sarah laughed. I looked at the still-empty stage over thousands of heads. I don't remember the concert.

Anne asked me where I'd been so long.

"It's Sarah's birthday today, I was invited to her house for lunch."

"Why didn't you tell me? I was worried."

"You know what? They had a big party with a delicious cake that her mother baked. So many presents she got, you should have seen how nicely they were wrapped."

I paused for a moment, and before I crawled under the covers in my room, I added,

"Yeah, and her mother sends her greetings."

Anne smiled and said that she should come visit us sometime, she could bake a cake, and we could drink tea together.

I could hardly wait for dinner.

Next day at school I wanted to ask Sarah if she and her mother would have time to visit us sometime. Where were they supposed to sit? On the bed where we slept? Her mother would not want to eat the cake that Anne made, it had too much chocolate and butter. Her mother was a very athletic woman, she even went jogging when it rained. I tried that once with Anne, after three minutes she stopped and smoked a cigarette. Then she wanted to keep jogging with the cigarette in her mouth.

Sarah's mother was allergic to cigarettes, she would suffocate at our place.

Then summer vacation came. I always woke up early, at the same time as Baba. In the bathroom there were two wash basins; I went to one, Baba to the other. Between the wash basins there was a black cassette player, and every morning Baba played the same cassette by Gülden Karaböcek and sang along softly. I knew every word, but I never sang along. He shaved, I washed my face. He combed his hair, I did too. He splashed lemon aftershave on his face, I put on lotion. When he finished and dried his hands, I did the same.

Then we went into the kitchen, where he made coffee for Anne.

Sarah had promised to call me as soon as they were back from vacation.

I ran into Simone on the street. I was astonished to see her, she went on vacation with Sarah and her family.

"How was your vacation? How long have you been back?"

Then I went on my way. Her words were spinning in my head.

"Two weeks already. I'm on my way to the swimming pool in Laupen with Sarah, what are you doing?"

The letter that would change our future arrived at the end of May 1995. We gave away our furniture, the orange bicycle, the parakeet, the rabbit family, the cat, the gerbils, and the idea of living in Switzerland.

We each packed a suitcase. We said goodbye to our neighbors, who stared at us in disbelief. The few friends we had gave us presents to take for their relatives, whom they had not seen in years. With the help of a friend who had been living in Switzerland longer and knew German better than he did, Baba wrote a letter to the school principal withdrawing my brother and me from school. Summer vacation was two weeks away, after that we would not go to that school any more.

When I came into the classroom on the last day, it got quiet.

"So children, now say goodbye. Please, slowly and properly, do you understand me?"

The teacher was standing in front of the blackboard.

One after another came to my desk and shook my hand. Some shook it, some clasped it firmly, some barely touched it, as though it made them sick.

No one looked me in the eye, I just heard a soft "Tschüss" every once in a while, more like a breath, Sarah was among those who shook my hand. She didn't want to cry in front of me, surely she would wait for me after school to say goodbye properly.

There were three "negatives" in all, that's what my parents called these letters.

The first negative was in a yellow envelope and shone out of the mailbox. I remember it clearly. In the whole letter I understood only that one word, "negative." I knew exactly what it meant. That was after we had lived in Switzerland four years. The second negative came after five years, and the third after six.

In my brother's class they had eaten cake that the teacher had baked for them and had fruit tea with it.

56

Everyone sang songs, he said, and all morning they watched movies.

I said that my class was sad, most had cried, hugged me, wished me all the best. We didn't watch movies, all morning we listened to music and danced. No one wanted me to leave.

Summer vacation was almost over, it had been raining for days. In a week we would travel to Prizren, the tickets were already on the table with our passports. When I emptied the mail box, there was a letter from the Commune in it. I gave it to Baba.

He knitted his eyebrows and called loudly for Anne.

I slid down the wall to the floor. My T-shirt rolled up my back and made a pad on my shoulders.

"Who's going to get our stuff back for us? We have nothing left here. They treat us like puppets."

I didn't move. The wall was cold on my back. I looked at my navel.

Baba shouted.

My legs were bent. They touched at the knees, my feet spread so wide apart I could see them to the left and right.

Anne straightened my T-shirt, drew me up by the arms, held my shoulders, and bent down to look me in the face.

"We're staying here, they've extended our residence permit. Are you glad?"

The first day of school after the summer vacation came closer, I dreaded the day. What was I supposed to say? How was I supposed to act? I had said goodbye to everyone. Now we were staying. I didn't want to stay. I wanted to go back to my friends, my family, my city. We stayed.

In the classroom I sat at a desk that no one else was using.

My bicycle was gone, so I went home on foot. I didn't like going on foot.

We had won the orange bicycle at an amusement park. Baba and Anne were walking behind us while we took off with the stroller. Baba bought a raffle ticket. All the prizes were on the table: fruit baskets, sausages, electric appliances, gift certificates, and lots more. My brother and I pushed through the crowd until we got right up front by the red table. We appraised every prize minutely. At the sight of one cake, my mouth filled with saliva, I swallowed. It was the same with my brother, a woman standing behind the table yelled,

"Hands off the cake, you can win it if you bought a ticket. Did you buy one?"

There was exactly enough for one ticket for the big raffle and one ride for me and my brother. We walked past every ride three or four times, watched the screaming people, compared the prices, listened to the music. I liked the colorful lights, I liked the laughing people. More than anything else I liked the fact that no one knew who I was.

We got into a shell with two seats attached to the end of the long tentacle of a pink octopus. When the man came and stretched out his big hand, I looked at my brother, because he had stuck the tickets in his pants pocket. He started to cry. The man passed his hand over his hair and signaled to us to keep quiet and not say anything.

"We were lucky again, you idiot!" I yelled at my brother.

The bright lights under the seats reflected on the metal floor. When it started, we screamed as loud as we could.

I tried to scream the German out of my head.

My hair fell over my face, I smelled the Pantene shampoo that Baba always bought, all our hair smelled the same. I held on so tight that my hands hurt. My brother shook his little head back and forth. We went up, came back down, the speed increased, the music drowned out our screams.

When we came to a stop, the German was still there.

"245! Who has number 245?" a woman's voice called out. That was us, that was our number. Someone pressed a big package into our hands; Baba put it on our stroller, so we went home not knowing what was in it. At home we unpacked the parts of the orange bicycle, and Baba screwed it together.

When they made fun of my bicycle, I rode past them real fast. I hummed a long, loud "hmm," then again softly, and then real loud; real loud and real long, while they yelled their incomprehensible sentences after me.

German was a disease, I tried not to think about it, it pursued me all day long. At some point I finally did understand the name-calling.

Now my bicycle was where we had been supposed to return to.

Mr. Lang has become a frail old man. What remains of his white hair he still combs over his bald spot.

He smiles and sets a bag on the old wooden counter behind which I sit, reading.

He carefully removes the heavy books from the bag, *Monuments of Switzerland*, which he's wrapped individually in white cloth.

"What are they worth? I'd like to sell them."

"These books are in almost every Swiss household. Unfortunately, we can't buy any more of them. If you like, you can leave the books here and I'll dispose of them."

"These are valuable books, you have no idea, I want to speak to the person in charge, a qualified person."

I explain to Mr. Lang that I'm that person and that I'm really sorry.

He stares at me without recognizing me, repacks his books, and leaves the used bookstore in the Old Town of Bern. You should have seen him. I sit down again and read *The Idiot*. The sun is shining again, it's getting warmer and warmer, the days are getting longer. The store windows are big, they let in a lot of light.

"In every other store the customer is king; in this store we're the kings."

I started my job with that statement by the owner. This used bookstore has been in business since 1955. It looks the same as it did then. The same furniture, the same cocomat carpet. The books organized alphabetically and by genre. The old dust gets into my clothing. The store extends from Kramgasse to Rathausgasse, it has two vaulted cellars and a large area for storing very valuable books. I will work here until the last day. Then we'll carry out the last boxes of books and make way for the construction site.

On the first day of summer vacation I had created a work space for myself in the attic.

Hot air streamed in through the only window. I put a table in the middle and sat with my back to the window. The room was small and separated from the rest of the attic by a door, it had served as a storage room for the kindergarten on the ground floor of this former schoolhouse. In the middle of the big attic room a thick rope hung from the ceiling, attached to a bell high above. Sometimes I tucked the knot in the end of the rope between my legs and rocked from side to side while the bell rang and hypnotized me.

We had filled the attic over the years. The broken TV was in the corner. I sat on the wooden floor in front of it and drew a line in the dust on the screen with my index finger.

"You smell like dust, whatever are you doing up there all day? Go to the swimming pool, it's hot out."

Anne didn't like my spending my vacation in the attic.

Herr Lang had told me before the summer vacation to prepare French lessons six, seven, and eight, otherwise he wouldn't let me go on to secondary school.

I had protested, I was just as far along as all the others, but he had insisted. I would have to show him my progress after the summer vacation, then promotion would be no problem.

Every day my alarm rang at seven a.m. I washed, got dressed, and went up to the attic. Every day I drew another line in the dust on the TV screen and wiped my finger off on my pant leg. I sat down at the desk and studied words, did exercises, read aloud, and wrote exams for myself. I had one notebook for the words that I had learned by heart, one for the tests I wrote, one for grammar, one for dictation, which I made my brother read to me, and one notebook for my drawings, when I couldn't study because my head ached.

When my brother and his friends came to see me in my chamber, to fetch me, I could not be persuaded and kept on studying until dark. Baba was the only one

61

who understood me. I should show this Mr. Lang, he said to me in his deep voice.

I would accomplish everything I set out to do, I was as pigheaded as he was. He brought food and home-made lemonade up to me, asked me words, tried to read French, which made us break out laughing.

On the last day of summer vacation I went into the attic room for the last time, sat down in front of the TV, and drew the forty-ninth line in the dust. The first one was scarcely recognizable anymore, I redrew all forty-nine.

On the first day of school, when I ran into Mr. Lang in the hallway, I tried to show him my notebooks.

"The secondary classes have already been made up, no further changes are possible."

I fly to Prizren to visit you.

Aga tells me a story. He always tells me a story when I see him.

"Once upon a time, never upon a time," he begins, sitting down on a large stone and wiping the sweat from his forehead. "On a Friday morning Ali was watering the flowers that grew in profusion from the earth beneath which his father's bones lay. On a wooden beam was written, Ali Baba, 1912–1992.

"A few meters away, Mehmet was sweeping dirt with a broom from a marble slab onto the graves beside it, which were almost invisible, discernible only by the stones hidden in the tall grass. On a gigantic black-marble slab, behind a pane of glass, was an engraved portrait of Mehmet's father: Mehmet Aga, 1912–1992.

"The marble beneath which Mehmet Aga's remains lay, likewise eaten by worms, was taller than all the other graves and remarkably clean.

"Mehmet asked Ali, 'Did your father mean so little to you that after he died you did not want to do him the honor of having a nice stone carved? Ali Baba was a good man, he left you so much money, you egoist.'

"Mehmet turned his back to Ali and walked away.

"'Poor Mehmet Aga,' Ali said to himself. 'When the Angel Gabriel blows his trumpet, you will have to make your way arduously through the hard ground out of your grave and then carry the heavy marble that your son gave you on your back for the journey. But my father will slip through the soft earth like a little worm, pluck a flower for himself, take the wooden board on his shoulder and float upward easily.'"

"Do you see all that marble over there?" Aga asks.

"The poor man will have to haul it, I tell you."

He points to an imposing grave stone, takes my arm, and smiles before we leave the cemetery.

The sun burns on my skin when Aga and I, on our way home, go into the bakery where I went with you every morning to get *kifle*.

Behind a blue curtain, hundreds of pieces of dough lie on a flour-covered table that is bigger than my bed. I watch the hands rolling the little pieces of floured dough into round, smooth balls between their palms and the wooden table. The hands roll the little balls in flour, slap them on the table, stroke them, as if they were stroking a child on the head. Then they get rolled into snakes, and the two ends are stuck together. The hands lay them on a large tin sheet and sprinkle them with sesame. The black door opens briefly and swallows the kifle.

"The dough must be soft as an earlobe."

The baker wipes his white sleeve across his forehead, takes the long, black shovel and sticks it into the fiery maw, rescuing the golden kifle before it burns.

He'd already pressed a kifle into my hand when I came in, and now he pinches my cheek until it starts to burn. I say "Thanks," softly, because there's kifle in my mouth.

I loved the sweet taste of the bread, which is why as a child I decided I would marry a baker, because I myself couldn't be one, since for years I had wanted to become a singer like Dragana Mirkovic.

Before the concert in the Domkultura in Prizren we were sitting in the front row, I went to the bathroom with Baba. I stood in front of the mirror and sang with an invisible microphone in my hand. When a woman came in the door, I ran out.

"Baba, I want to meet Dragana Mirkovic."

Baba took me by the hand down a long hallway. He said I had to be quiet. We snuck through the hallways.

"If my daughter wants to meet Dragana Mirkovic, she will meet Dragana Mirkovic."

We burst into a room, and two men came toward us to throw us out. Baba defended himself, spoke in Dragana Mirkovic's language, yelled at the men, pointed to me. Dragana made a pretty gesture with her hand, and the men let us go.

I showed off the imprint of her red lips after she kissed me on the cheek until Anne made me take a bath.

"How many kifles should we get, are you very hungry?" Aga asks.

The baker wraps ten in a piece of paper before putting them into a thin plastic bag.

Aga knows everyone in Prizren. After the war, the textile factories, Printeks and Perlonka, the preserves manufacturer Progres, Farmakos, and the gold and silver factory Famipa were closed, thousands of people lost their jobs, among them my Aga. He had worked for Famipa for twenty years.

His old-age pension plan, which he had paid into for twenty years, disappeared into thin air after the war. He's seventy years old.

For a few years he's worked for Eagle TV, a pay-TV company.

Every day he rides his bicycle through the area, a notepad with names and addresses in his pocket, and collects five euros per month from every household with digital service. After drinking a coffee, he crosses off the people's names in his book. Aga must drink fifty coffees a day.

"That's the daughter of my brother—my brother's daughter—the daughter of my brother—daughter of my brother—brother's daughter—my brother, his daughter."

Always the same words and sentences beneath the burning sun.

One bead of sweat after another runs down Aga's forehead, and he wipes it away with his hand, from which half of his little finger is missing, and wipes it off on his pant leg. When he was building his house, which he has been doing since 1983, he sawed off his fingertip.

"I saw the fingertip lying on the ground, threw it in the garbage, stuck the bleeding finger in raki, bandaged it, and kept on working."

Aga is a strong man who cannot live alone. After his wife, who was present at my birth in the little room in the little house of my grandparents opposite Aga's house, where my cousin lives—after she got diabetes and died of it, Aga married again, one year later, so that he would not have to die alone.

In Aga's house everyone talked at the same time. He always put on the same record of Coşkun Sabah, danced to it while he sang along loudly. He reminded me of my doll at home, which I could turn on with a button, then Turkish music came out of the holes in its back, she moved her hips and turned around in circles. No, there was no more music, and she didn't move her hips any more, and she had not turned in circles for a long time. My brother, when he had barely begun to crawl, dragged everything along with him. First, one of my T-shirts on his little shoe. He kept on crawling. A doll, whose long hair got tangled in his pant leg. He kept on crawling. My pink blanket in his left hand, a fire truck in the right. If he'd kept crawling, he'd have taken the whole house with him. Unfortunately, his travels usually ended with my toys. He sat in his full diapers, his legs spread out, picked up one doll after another, took off their little dresses, twisted their arms and legs, took their heads off, and gaped in astonishment into the dark holes. That's how I found him. I yelled so loudly that he began to cry. Anne came and took him into her arms. She left the room with him giving me a reproachful look.

Aga still danced, unlike my doll. I glared at my brother, who was pushing a little car back and forth on the floor, then he grabbed his pillow and fell asleep under the table.

There were pictures everywhere in carefully selected frames. I knew them all, I always looked at them again and again.

One in particular: We had all got dressed up, Babaanne on a chair in the middle, the little ones in front, the big ones in back. Babaanne was starting her pilgrimage to Mecca on that day. Like Aga a few years later. After that I should have called him Haci Aga. To celebrate the day we had prepared a small meal with a hundred of our closest friends. In the photo I was in front between my brother, who was scratching his leg, and Ismail, who was adjusting the glasses on his nose. I was wearing a red dress, had folded my arms, and was looking at the camera not very happily. We were photographed so often on that day that I simply had no more desire to smile. Babaanne was sitting on her chair with a stern look, Dede was standing next to her, smiling. Anne was only partly visible, my aunt's hairdo hid half of her face. Baba was probably about to say something, Aco was looking at him instead of looking into the camera.

At Aga's there was always the same thing to drink. For adults, coffee or tea, for the little ones, strawberry juice. I liked fresh strawberries best. In June, when the first ones turned red among the green in the garden, Dede picked a bowlful and sprinkled sugar over them. We sat silently beside each other on the veranda and ate the sweet, crystal-dusted redness.

Aga's strawberry juice did not taste like strawberries. I tried to hold it in my mouth as long as possible. Anne glared at me till I had swallowed it all.

When I heard Baba say it was time to go home, I pretended to be asleep. Two arms reached for me, picked me up. The lemon scent of his aftershave told me it was Baba. I heard Anne say,

"You know she's not asleep, she should walk by herself, put her down."

From Baba's mouth I heard only a soft,

"Not so loud, my girl's sleeping."

I kept my eyes closed until we were on the street, then I opened them slowly. Over his shoulder the world looked different, with every step it moved up and down gently. His neck was warm, his hair felt cool on my forehead. My brother walked holding Anne's hand. What a dummy, I thought.

Their footsteps echoed far into the night. It was dark, no one was to be seen, only a cat ran quickly across the yellow-lit street, stopped in the middle of it, and looked at me with green eyes. For fear that it might divine my secret and betray me to my parents, I closed my eyes quickly.

When Babaanne returned from Mecca, she was Haci Babaanne. She brought gold jewelry, fabrics, clothing, and kina.

I'm running through the tall grass to the fountain. Slowly I strip off my headscarf with my wet hand and put it into my handbag after I wash my face with cold water.

I had washed and put on fresh clothes before I phoned Hasan. I put the headscarf and prayer book into my handbag. I could have gone on foot, but I was afraid that I'd have to go to the bathroom on the way. When you've washed yourself for prayers, you're not supposed to go to the bathroom, otherwise you have to wash yourself all over again. So I sat in the taxi and focused and didn't say a word. Just before I got out I pulled the white headscarf over my hair. The long pants and long-sleeve sweater soon made me sweat.

"Can you wait here?" I asked Hasan.

I went into the cemetery and prayed three *kulhuvallahs* and one *elham* for all the dead lying there before I walked through the weed-overgrown graves to Baba's grave.

"Allah kabul etsin kizim—may God hear your prayer, my girl," said Hasan, who waits for me at the entry gate.

I visit you every day for a week.

Every day, Hasan drives me to the cemetery and waits for me.

After one week I fly back to Anne.

When the doorbell rings, I'm in the shower. I hear Anne go to the door, pick up the receiver of the intercom, and ask too loudly who's there.

Then she pushes the green button to open the building entry. She opens the apartment door, and a voice reverberates through the seventh floor. I'm still in the shower, listen to the discussion, understand nothing, and keep on taking my shower.

Anne comes into the bathroom, sits down on the closed toilet seat lid.

"There was a man here selling cookies and homemade cards."

One leg crosses over the other, her foot describing circles of different sizes in the air, like dissipating smoke rings. I look at her, she can't see me. Her hands grope for the terry-cloth towel that I've asked for.

"Lower down, a little more to the left, no farther down, yes, that one. I'm here, can you hear me? To the right, thanks."

Anne had to leave her feet beside each other on the ground, that's what her Anaanne, her mother, my other grandmother advised her to do.

"In a wedding dress, the bride does not cross her legs, that's indecent."

Anne was twenty-two years old. On May 23, 1982, she had menstrual cramps, it was her wedding day.

An old gold coin and a mint soothed the pain. The whole day she had to sit on a chair without crossing her legs, which was as hard for her as not smoking, for she was not allowed to smoke, either. Baba's family picked her up in a decorated car, with Romas, music, and many tears. The father of the bride passed the bride to the father of the groom. The bride got into the car, and the groom drove her home to his family, her new family, to her new house. Hundreds of people were already there, dancing and waiting for the bride. The bride was placed on a decorated throne and looked downward demurely while the others danced, drank, ate, and partied. Her made-up face was covered with a veil, leaving her beauty to the imagination. Anne's stomach growled, the pain in her body tormented her, the gold coin tasted metallic, the mints had run out, she was not allowed to speak. Her dowry was in the room to which she was led at the end of the day, to the groom, who had been chased through the whole city and had been driven into the room with blows. They were locked in the room, the guests partied on outside until they had changed and came out of the room and received guests for a whole month, every day, Anne in a new, tailor-made dress. After ten months I came into the world in that room, and for another five years we lived in it until Anne and Babaanne, who had not gotten along from the beginning, began to fight, and we moved out.

I dry my wet body.

"Did you wash thoroughly? *Gusul abdes* is important before prayers. Can I brush your hair? Where's your head? How was Prizren?"

Anne gets up, she's a head shorter than I am, caresses my hair with her hands, feels for the brush, and begins at the ends.

"It's grown, your hair. When you were a child, it was always very long after I washed it. When it was dry, it curled so much that you had a short haircut."

A strip of bare skin sticks to the cold leather of the sofa. I lean forward and push the play button on the Sony player, which took us years to pay off. Finally the skin comes unstuck, and I pull my T-shirt down over my hips.

I'm sitting between my brother and sister, holding the prayer book so that both can read along with me.

With the index finger of my other hand I trace the lines. Anne is sitting across from us and prays with the green prayer beads that you used every Friday morning to pray for your parents. From the Sony box a male voice prays the *Yasin* in the Arabic language. We repeat after it, following the Latin letters. The praying male voice drowns us out as we murmur along with it, softly and not quite correctly. My brother scratches his head, I look at him and back to the prayer book. My sister isn't reading along properly, I point to the word emphatically, she whispers a little louder.

My brother jabs me with his elbow. I try to turn the page, the paper sticks, I lick my finger with my tongue, my brother pokes me again, this time harder, I look for the word that the male voice is speaking, rub my aching upper arm, find the line again, the whispering continues. My sister yawns, I poke her with my elbow, my brother pokes me, I poke him, and Anne says simultaneously with the male voice, "Amen."

"Amen," we murmur too.

On my brother's fifth birthday I rushed home from school, through the narrow streets, past Mustafa's store and the little park with the fountain. There was torte, the torte we always had, the best torte, filled with chocolate, vanilla crème, strawberries, raspberries, banana slices, and more chocolate poured over it. The TV was on and Sinan Sakic was dancing and singing on a stage.

When the doorbell rang, Anne ran to the door. A man stretched out both hands, he kept his head down so that I couldn't make out his face. Anne reached for his hands, straightened him up, smiled at him, and made him wait in the doorway for a moment and disappeared into the kitchen, then into the bedroom, then into the bathroom, then once more into the bedroom, then again into the kitchen. She was like a whirlwind, her hair streaming behind as though it couldn't keep up.

I watched her and forgot about the man. Anne rushed back to the door with two bags filled with homemade jam, cake, bread, Baba's clothing, soap, lemon water, and I don't know what all. The young man was gone.

Anne ran barefoot out onto the veranda, she had just painted her toenails red, she hung over the railing, looking left and right. The wind blew her dress. Then she came back in and began to unpack the two bags.

"That was an angel who came disguised as a beggar to test our generosity. There are a great many angels, most of them are beggars, never forget that, and leave no hand empty. Even if you have nothing, fill the hand with the warmth of your own, and if you don't have food or money, give him a smile."

Later that evening Anne takes a CD out of her handbag and we listen to Sinan Sakic, sit on the balcony on the seventh floor, and look out over Bümpliz.

She asks me to dance. I laugh and look at her. Anne moves her hips, her hair dances one way, her body the other.

"Can I let my hair grow more? It's gotten so thin with the years. Do I have a lot of white hairs?"

I like Anne best laughing and dancing.

Most of the time I don't like her much.

"Children, please write your names and phone numbers legibly on this yellow sheet of paper so that I can start the telephone tree if the May Walk doesn't happen."

Everyone in the classroom was yelling wildly at the same time, so they could barely understand the teacher. Melanie was crying because she had taken the mouse out of the cage and dropped it, Lukas was making little paper balls and throwing them at the back of my head, one after another. Martin laughed every time Lukas hit me. Andreas was eating chocolate and licking his thick fingers off. My heart beat faster every time the yellow sheet was passed on, until finally it lay before me and Andreas was staring at it as though it were a piece of lemon cake. "Fifth Grade, Neuenegg" was written on it in the upper left-hand corner. I wrote my name under Andreas's and quickly passed the sheet on.

"She didn't write her phone number, she didn't write her phone number."

I was so excited before the first day of school in Neuenegg, I had put on pretty clothes and let my curly hair fall down my back. Almost a year had passed during which I had not gone to school. My brother was placed in the kindergarten, and I was assigned to the third grade. Baba accompanied us to the schoolhouse.

There were lots of shoes under the bench in the hallway. We were late, Baba held my hand tight and knocked on the door. A woman with short brown hair and round glasses on her nose opened it, and we looked into the classroom. The sun through the row of windows was blinding. The woman came toward us and spoke to Baba, who said yes to everything and nodded without understanding a word. Then she took me by the hand and said something that I didn't understand, either, and Baba kept nodding and repeating his yeses. Blond girls with smooth, shoulder-length hair. The boys in pressed T-shirts and jeans. A whispering wafted through the warm room like a cold draft. I had put on blue bib overalls and red patent-leather shoes that Dede bought for me from the old cobbler before we came to Switzerland. At recess I went into the bathroom to wet my hair so that I could tie it back more easily so that no one could see how long and curly it was. And to hide. I was a year older than everyone else in my class, I had to repeat the third grade because of the language.

I wanted to go back to Prizren. Back there, where my best friend Gül came by for me every morning. Her mother brushed her long hair and tied it together for her. We walked to school together hand in hand, singing, and played with the others in the schoolyard. When the bell rang, we all ran into the pink building. Each of us sat in our place, and when the teacher came into the room, we all stood up and said in unison,

"Günaydin ögretmenim."

"Günaydin cocuklar," she replied, and we sat down with folded arms on our little chairs. The teacher came by each desk to inspect our hands, ears, and mouths. Not even the freshly ironed handkerchief could be missing. One day I left my notebook at home and had to go to the front of the room to the teacher. She got a long, wooden ruler out of the drawer, I knew exactly what was coming. I held out my right hand to her, my tensely squeezed fingertips upward, my eyes shut tight, and waited for the sharp pain. That short moment seemed to last an eternity, so long that a thought was able to squeeze in between the waiting and the pain. I should have brought the apple instead of the banana. No, an apple is better. But a banana tastes good, too. I thought that, and the thought was interrupted by the hard blow of the ruler on my finger tips. Good thing I have an apple, because I would not have been able to peel a banana. I did not make a sound and went back to my place. Everyone was still and watched me. I sat down on my chair, gripped my right hand with the left one behind the backrest and squeezed it hard, trying to squeeze the pain away.

"Never, I'll never ever forget anything again," I said to Gül. She laughed as though she didn't believe a single word. I laughed, too, not because of Gül but because I was glad I had an apple.

Then a loud beeping jars me out of that memory.

My brother's face appears on my cell phone. It vibrates loudly, so many in the auditorium turn around toward me. I turn off the cell phone, put it into my bag. A woman sitting beside me has the attendance list for the lecture and lays it down in front of me. I can't decide what I want to study. I go to so many lectures that I no longer know which ones interest me and which do not and go to them again and again until a year passes and you're still gone.

I write my name on it and pass it on. No one knows me, I don't know anyone. On the blackboard it says,

"Adults commit a barbaric sin when they destroy children's creativity by robbing them of their world, suffocate it under traditional, dead knowledge, and conform it to specific goals that are foreign to it."

I look around. Lots of people are sitting there, paying more or less attention to the professor. A woman beside me is playing a computer game, the man in front of me is reading comics on his laptop, others are writing down what the professor says. I write down my thoughts on a piece of paper.

Suddenly I notice my face in the polished window pane, staring at me. It's gotten dark. A high-pitched voice comes from the white boxes high up in the corners of the room. My hands are on the table. A pigeon flutters outside the window, forcing my gaze past the reflection of the professor, past the many heads, through myself, to the outside. The broad street, bathed in white light, lies beneath me. It is indistinct, branches out, seems infinite. Little colored lights flash, some of them very brightly. They move as one. My eyes focus on the reflection again. The professor floats above the lights. Someone opens the window, I disappear over the street.

When I got home, Anne was looking out the window and called, "Come on, come on, we're all waiting for you, hurry, go, faster."

Everyone was sitting silently on the sofa. On the table lay the phone book for 1997. Baba motioned to me, tapped lightly on the space beside him, took the phone book, opened it, and looked for a name. I raised my eyebrows. My sister was sitting on Baba's lap, and Anne had her arm around my brother, who was staring at the book excitedly.

I exhaled loudly, was about to get up and leave, when Baba's finger came to a stop at a name. Our heads bumped together. There it was, our name was in the phone book.

We screamed, my sister hopped up and down without knowing why. Anne hopped with her, my brother hopped with them, Baba hugged me, turned up the music coming from the TV, and asked me to dance. Then the phone rang.

The next day at school I prayed for a phone list. I had learned the phone number by heart overnight.

I lie in the empty bathtub, water flows over my knees, creeps between my toes, surrounds my feet, caresses my legs, lies on my stomach, covers my chest, tickles my chin. I submerge my head in the warm water, breathe out through my nose, my gaze follows the bubbles rising to the condensation on the ceiling. The shower curtain moves through the ripples. The ceiling becomes the floor, as though I were floating. My water-borne hair obscures my sight, I try vainly to free my face. I surface hastily and take a deep breath. My hands look like Babaanne's.

Baba went out to phone Babaanne. The phone booth was at the post office in Wilderswil, five minutes from the old hotel. Baba got ever smaller until he disappeared completely. I didn't move, I stayed at the window until I saw him getting bigger again. A point, a line, a person, a man, Baba was back.

I ran from the room, down the steps, through the big room to the entry door. Baba went by without seeing me, through the big room, up the stairs, into the room. He moved slowly, I followed him hastily. When he closed the door in my face, I stood in front of it for awhile, then I opened it carefully. I saw Baba sitting on the bed, his hands covering his face.

"Babaane is dead."

It was a voice I had never heard before. It was a sentence I had never heard before.

I went into the bathroom and shut myself in. I let the water run in the bathtub so that I couldn't hear anything more about death. In the dark, a ray of light shone through the keyhole, and I caught the light in the palm of my hand. I recalled the last story that Babaanne told me.

"Once upon a time, never upon a time, there was a mighty king who had a son who was very sick. One day he heard about a woman who could cure the ill with her touch. He ordered two of his servants to take his son and go to the miracle healer.

"'Woe betide you if you do not bring my son back cured.'

"The men set out on the long journey. After two days the child died. They were afraid to report this to the king. One man stepped forward from the multitude and said he would tell the king. Surprised, they asked him whether he was not afraid of being beheaded. He shook his head and set out on his way to the king.

"On the day he arrived, the entire village was gathered before the king, each was allowed to ask for advice. The man waited a long time before he was allowed to come forward. Before the assembled throng he said,

"'Sire, a long time ago a good friend gave me a gift, now he wants the gift back.'

"'Did you pay for this gift or sign something?'

"'No.'

"'If you paid nothing nor signed anything then you are not the owner and must give the gift back to your friend.'

"'Then I have one more question, my king. When your son came into this world, did you pay anything or sign anything?'

"'No, of course not.'

"'He is back where he came from.'

"The man went through the crowd and left the hall."

With wet feet I drag my heavy body before the fogged mirror, which shows a woman's body blurrily. On the steamed-up mirror, her index finger with red nail polish connects the birth marks on her upper body. Cassiopeia appears, drowning in the sea and crying for help. Through the lines that have been drawn on the mirror the view is clearer. A cool breeze blows through the open window and carries the fog out into the night. Cassiopeia is only barely visible.

The view in the clear mirror shows me.

"In the name of merciful and gracious God."

Babaanne read from the Koran constantly, so it seemed to me. On a pillow on her lap. She read in the Arabic language, the language of Mohammed. My language it's not. She wore a white headscarf and covered her long, black hair. She repeated short prayers until I began to repeat them, too.

She sat on the low seat cushion, I on the patterned rug. She kept on praying after I had already left. I repeated the prayers on the street, in the car, in bed, on my chair until my brother repeated them under the table on his pillow.

Babaanne bent forward, crooking her back as though she were about to fall into the great book. Through the glasses sitting on the tip of her nose I could see the many Arabic letters. The letters got smaller when I looked through the glasses.

"Why do you have glasses if they make the letters smaller than they really are?"

"That's not how it is. When I wear them, I see the letters bigger."

I put on the glasses and an old hat, which Babaanne said she got from her grandfather, and twirled in circles until it made me nauseous and I landed on the soft carpet. I loved the feeling of dizziness, even though it didn't last long. I wanted to keep twirling as long as the dervishes did; not fall down, and in no case lose control. It made me dizzy to watch the dervishes on TV.

I sat down with her again. I still did not understand a word. She kept praying, and I went to the bathroom.

I knew that you're not allowed to say any Arabic words in the bathroom, because it's a sacred language that all Muslims were supposed to speak, but never in the bathroom; that would foul the language with the stench, and anyway God had no business in the bathroom.

So I stopped reciting the prayers in the bathroom, but I did at school, on the way home, in the library, in bed. Every morning I put my right foot on the floor first, said "bismillahi rahmani rahim," went into the bathroom, washed my face, since if I didn't wash, I was not allowed to eat. I was allowed to eat only with my right hand, to greet or to say goodbye to someone only with my right hand, and to leave the house with my right foot and whisper "bismillahi rahmani rahim." One is allowed to use the left hand only in the bathroom.

It was a lot that I had to think about. That's why I forgot to feed my brother, wash my hands, go home after school, bring my school notebooks, put on my shoes, not chew on my pencils. Once I forgot how to untie a knot. I had tied a string tightly around by brother's neck, so tight that he could hardly breathe. Anne came and cut his breath loose.

Our parents showed us off to friends and neighbors till they all clapped their hands. My brother and I recited our verses in our pretty clothes.

The words catch up with me twenty years later, I repeat them, bring them back into my mouth, speak them through my lips, and still do not understand them.

"We had elephants in our yard. The smallest one stuck his head through the window into my room and wanted me to feed him nuts."

"Dumbo? Like the elephant in the cartoon?"

"Exactly, that was his name, the name fit him perfectly. I wanted a giraffe, too, but my father thought it would grow too big and look over the roofs so that our neighbors could see it, and we wanted to keep our animals secret so that no one could take them away from us."

"Why would someone take your animals away? Did you bring the animals with you to Switzerland in your suitcases?"

Sarah was skeptical of my stories. Every time I told her about my home, she asked me lots of questions.

"We even had a lion in the yard, he was dangerous, he protected us from burglars. Once, the lion attacked my grandfather, but he could take care of himself. He had been in a thousand wars, a lion was nothing compared to that. After that attack, my grandfather only had ripped trousers, otherwise he was in one piece."

"You had a lion as a pet?"

I couldn't stop, I didn't have anything else to tell, nothing about our vacation or cool birthday presents or trips with our grandparents. What was I supposed to tell about after vacation, when Herr Lang asked in French class what exciting things we'd done? Was I supposed to say my parents had smoked and fought so much because they spent the whole day together? That they were not allowed to work and yelled at us and worried every day? Or that I was lonely because no one phoned me, that I was bored? Or maybe how many times I cried and missed my cousins and girlfriends?

"The lion—that was his name, too, Lion, I didn't have any other name for him—after he fought with my grandfather, the lion became gentle, even played with me and my brother in the yard. We didn't have to be afraid anymore, I think my grandfather whispered something in his ear, a name, maybe, the way you do with little children, to give them their names, you whisper their names in their ears three times. The lion must have been mad that we didn't give him a name."

I had barely finished that sentence when Raphael, the scout camp counselor, came into the tent and forbade us to talk and laugh. We were supposed to go to sleep.

I'm walking down Marktgasse and run into Sarah. She looks the same as ever. If I hadn't seen Sarah for twenty years, I would recognize her. I've changed. My hands are bigger.

Sarah is reserved, as always. In the hug we give each other in greeting, I'm the one who squeezes harder. She hasn't much time, she has to keep going, she says at the beginning, in a voice so soft it seemed as if meant to protect my ears. But doesn't she have time to go for a tea with me? She doesn't have time, she repeats, smiling, as though I can't take the truth.

"Let's get together sometime. I would love to see you again. We haven't talked in such a long time, I meant to phone you. I've been working so much lately, and I moved again. Come see me, I would really like that."

I say, "yes" and hold her tight.

I catch myself imitating her laugh.

As a child I sat in front of the TV or radio for hours and listened. My TV German did not go over well with the pupils, we were in Switzerland, not Germany.

The palms of her hands pat my back lightly, I rub hers hard.

Sarah smells like curd soap, like a baby, she doesn't wear perfume. I smell like smoke; I come from a meeting with Ruth.[1] Ruth talks with her hands, sometimes she closes her eyes while she talks. I can see her eyeballs moving back and forth under the lids. Her hands

---

[1]Ruth Schweikert, Swiss author of *Augen zu* (*Close Your Eyes*).

conduct her rough voice, sound waves that penetrate the haze and come into my ears. I noticed her long fingers and their long nail beds at our very first meeting. I always wanted long nail beds. She has a wool blanket around her hips, her light hair is behind her ears. The room is small, hot, and smoky. A mattress, a table, books, and smoke fill it until there's no more space.

Sarah doesn't know Ruth, I give her *Augen zu* to read. She says she'll give it back to me when I visit her.

"I'll call you next week," Sarah says, and vanishes into the arcades.

I go into the Münstergass Bookstore and buy the book that I gave Sarah. I won't see her again, some day our paths will happen to cross, she will hug me, she'll say I should come visit her, she will smile at me and smell of curd soap, she'll say she has one of my books, she'll say I should call her, I'll call, she won't call back.

In the middle of the night I was torn from sleep with a cry, my eyes were blindfolded, I was driven through the woods barefoot in my pajamas. My breath kept time with my steps. No one else was there. I had to follow a stretched rope blindfolded. The blindfold over my eyes smelled like puke. A male voice said loudly that I was not allowed to remove the blindfold under any circumstances, that I had to go through this, it was part of the initiation.

Florian, all because of Florian. I hated sleeping in the tent, going to the bathroom in the woods, bathing in the cold river, singing with a group and clapping our hands.

He knew nothing of my love for him. Why should I reveal my feelings to him? He would not have fallen in love with someone like me, he fell in love with Anninas, Sarahs, and Manuelas.

Florian, it's definitely Florian. He's sitting in the bus beside me. I can see him only from the side. He still looks exactly like he did in fourth grade. Florian is blond, well built, has long lashes, fine hands; he probably works in an office. He's wearing dark jeans and a black jacket, like most do. I'm sitting by the window, he looks out past me. Then he says my name questioningly in my direction. We look at each other. He repeats my name. I say, "Yes, Florian."

His eyes move from my left eye to my right one, down to my nose, on to my mouth, which is made up red with the new lipstick I just bought. I'm afraid I've colored not just my lips but my teeth, too, and run my tongue carefully over my front teeth with my mouth closed. He probably sees that my upper lip bulges from left to right and back again. It must look funny, I stop immediately and make a forced smile. He looks at my neck.

I keep smiling with an effort, and behind my hand I wipe my teeth with my index finger until they get quite dry and I have to make a bulge again in order to speak without having my upper lip stick to my teeth.

Maybe he's married and already has children. Maybe he loves someone else.

The taut rope ended at a tree. The wind moved some branches, ants crawled on my feet. It smelled of rain-drenched earth and a little like the air, like when you come home from the woods and smell like the air.

I heard steps, they got louder and faster. I turned around with a scream and someone knocked me to the ground with a hard shove.

When I came to, I thought I'd been asleep for a couple of hours. I had dreamed, too, I just couldn't remember what. The images were clear, but when I tried to remember them, everything disappeared.

My eyes still blindfolded, I felt a hand helping me to get up. It led me out of the woods. The walk ended at the lake. There they removed the blindfold. Everything was blurry.

I give Florian my telephone number.

"Swim! Go! Get in, to the red ball and back. Now, quick."
I could not react at all, I was already standing up to my knees in ice-cold Lake Constance, another shove from behind and I fell in. The cold deadened my body. My hands felt as though they were swollen. The long lake hair wrapped around my legs. Water got into my ears, eyes, nose. I lay outstretched in the waves, which supported me, but before I could fall asleep, I came up.
The world was still blurry. I tried to free my face from the long green hair. I swam to the red point and back. The blurry world gradually came back into focus. I saw a fire, everyone was sitting around it, Florian covered me with a blanket, I sat down by the fire beside him and had to drink something made of pepper, spit, lake water, weeds, sand, and I don't know what else, then I had to shout my initiation name "Mocca" at the world three times.

A few minutes after I get off the bus, Florian sends me a text message. I won't contact him.

I have never not been in love. The first boy who loaned me his pencil, the boy who asked my name, the one who shared a roll with me, and the one with whom all the other girls were in love. Later I fell in love with the man who held a door open for me, with the one who wished me happy birthday, with the one who was my best friend, with the one who said what pretty eyes I had, with the one who had a light blue shirt, with the one with the lightning quick wit, with the one who took me out to dinner, with the one who recommended a book to me, with the one who unexpectedly kissed me on a park bench, and with others in between. In most cases, though, I kept it to myself.

I will fall in love with a man who wears his glasses crooked, behind which hide the bluest of eyes. He will leave his small change lying around everywhere, he will sketch me, on the third day, on the train, he will confess his love. He will kiss me.

You won't meet him.

While you were kissing me, a tear dropped from the tip of my nose to your cheek and cried on your face to the end.

Dede kissed me.

Dede didn't kiss like all the others who kissed me. When he kissed me, he smelled me.

"Biliyormusun, I breathe a little of you into my heart, there you will remain for a long time. Every time I breathe out, a little of you escapes."

I felt the cold of the outdoors on my cheek.

"You are a song that never ends. I would die without this melody."

"What happens when a person dies?" I asked him, because until now only animals that I knew had died.

"We must all die some day. The older people first, so Babaanne and I, then your parents, and you only at the end. Dying is like a journey on which you see everyone again who traveled before you."

"You must not die without me. It doesn't matter to me when I have to die, you must never die. Take back what you said, take it back immediately."

"Have some sugar, then you'll feel better."

We looked at the moon in the sky, which looked exactly as I drew it.

Your coffin was carried through the town. The funeral procession began with ten people and ended with a large gathering. Women turned off their stoves and walked along for a while. Men closed their shops and walked along for a while. Children stopped playing ball and walked along for a while. All were quiet and walked along for a while. Death is taken for a walk almost every day in Prizren.

The men with whom you went to mosque in Bern washed your corpse and shrouded it in the seven meters. That's how it's done. You were laid in a coffin of wood, which was nailed shut. Your brothers would want to see your face through a glass pane, the *hoca* said.

I waited outside until the men were done, then I left before they carried the coffin away.

You flew with us, under us, in the baggage compartment.

In Prizren your photo was everywhere, the burial was set for the next day. I lay down to sleep in the little room.

The next morning I stood at the window in Aga's house while your brothers carried your coffin into your parents' house, through the yard where you played as a child, married Anne, and where I took my first steps.

In the next room, a hundred people gathered to pray for you. When the hoca with the high-pitched voice began to spit into the microphone, I was the only one who broke out in laughter. My aunt angrily pulled me out of the room by the arm. You would have laughed, too.

After the burial I lay down on the moist earth and imagined my tears seeping through the earth and landing on your face, one after another.

The cemetery is in the town. A wall protects its inhabitants. Next to the Turkish-Islamic cemetery is the Ottoman one. There's been a wall around it for a few years; at the entrance, a German-speaking watchman makes sure that people remember.

"Seven times a day you should think about death."

Dede talked about death a lot.

Dede went for a walk one Friday afternoon, where he probably met death. He came home, got tired, and lay down to die.

He always told me the same story, the story of the caterpillar. The caterpillar, which must endure an arduous life, moves very slowly, lives in fear of being eaten, constantly looks for food, gets caught in a sheath, then lies down to die and is reborn as a butterfly.

All the children were sitting in a circle, we held hands and sang songs. I understood hardly anything, and when the word "hallelujah" came, I kept quiet.

I thought that if I said that word, I would go to the hell for Muslims.

In every room there were large wooden crosses on the walls, which I didn't look at. After eating, we had to fold our hands, close our eyes, and pray. Ben had dirty fingernails, Sophie chewed on a strand of blond hair, and Martina moved her little finger up and down as though setting the tempo. Joel, the camp counselor, scratched his forehead with his folded hands and then rested his nose on his thumbs.

I couldn't get to sleep that night, it was dark, and I watched the moon, hoping it would shine my fear away. I forced myself to think of the funny ducks, which I often watched on the river. I tried to laugh. The ducks stuck their green, blue, black, and brown heads with yellow beaks in front into the water, moved their orange feet as fast as they could to keep their rear ends above the water. I felt hungry because the meatless food didn't taste good to me. While everyone had their eyes closed to pray, I spit the well-chewed food into a napkin and later clogged the toilet with it.

I was also afraid of going to hell when I wanted to fast for half the day in the month of Ramadan and during handicrafts put the thread into my mouth to make it go through the eye of the needle better. I definitely wanted to fast, but Anne had forbidden me to fast the whole day; I was too young, so I was allowed to fast only half the day. Nothing to eat from after lunch until evening. I walked to school past the bakery. How I would have loved to buy a chocolate roll with my two francs. The second hand in the needlework classroom went more slowly than ever. I tried to finish sewing the etui. There were only a few stitches to go. The bell rang for the first recess. Sarah pulled chocolate, an apple, and a piece of bread out of her school bag. I pretended to look through my bag for the chocolate roll that I hadn't bought. The letter that my parents had not understood came out. I definitely wanted to go to the camp where Florian was going, too. I lied to my parents that it was a school camp and everyone had to go. Florian got sick shortly before, and every day I had to live with the fear of going to hell.

"Would you like a bite?"

Saliva pooled under my tongue. Time did not pass, and I would not finish my etui in two hours. At home it smelled of food. Everything was quiet when we sat down at the table to pray. After dinner I was as proud of myself as if I had dived five meters. The feeling I had while I was eating was like the feeling of coming up for air.

The sky is blue, a big truck with "Honegger" written on it drives by.

Blue is the color of the eye on a gold chain around my sister's neck that has kept watch ever since she was born.

I look at my brother, see you in his face, watch the green lettering pass by, and look back to my brother. We're sitting in Adrianos near the *Zytglogge*, the Clock Tower, drinking *caffè freddo*. He's grown a beard. His hair is curly and black. He's become a man.

My brother had not been back to the airport in three years because he doesn't have a valid ID, which is why he can't travel to Pristina to have a new passport issued. The Serbian embassy has been promising to send him a new passport for three years, my brother doesn't speak Serbian, and they don't like it if someone who is not Serbian applies for a Serbian passport.

When my brother is at the airport to pick up Anne, who comes out of the plane with her cane accompanied by man or a woman, the police always take him into a room and interrogate him and demand ID, but he has no ID and no passport, and they won't release him, and Anne waits for him, worrying, and when they release him after a few hours and don't apologize for it, my brother can pick up Anne, who has been waiting alone among all those people, imagining the worst has happened.

Early in the morning, before anyone is up, I hear Anne crying. Early in the morning you were up making coffee for Anne. Back then I awoke to the aroma of coffee, now her crying wakes me. I can't comfort her. What am I supposed to do? Every moment I'm not with her, my conscience torments me. I'm furious because she makes me feel how lonely she is. Sometimes I have to shut myself in the bathroom to catch my breath. Then I tell her that I don't understand her, and she says,

"None of you understand me, and you speak a different language than I do. Switzerland has turned us into strangers."

The truck with the green inscription moves very slowly. My sister laughs, probably about what my brother is saying.

Baba spent many a night cleaning airplanes as an employee of the Honegger Company, while Anne waited for him with sleep in her face. Sometimes he was given cleaning agents and cloths that could absorb liters of water without getting wet, and he talked about the cleaning agents as if they were superheroes.

Baba cleaned airplanes, offices, schoolhouses, libraries, stores, chandeliers, cars, refrigerators, living rooms, floors, toilets, garbage cans, gymnasiums, kitchens, coffee machines, carpets, musical instruments, classrooms, movie theaters, and dead Muslims before they were laid in the ground, and then he cleaned the table they had been lying on.

I'm envious of the ring that my sister got from Anne for her fourteenth birthday. A gold ring with a little flower that Anne's uncle from Istanbul made for her when she turned fourteen. Only when I get married will I get the gold chain that Anne always wears around her neck, which she got from her mother when she got married. When Anne is not wearing it, I try it on, it hangs almost to my belly button, and the pendant is the size of the circle that my thumb and forefinger make when I bring the tips together. A flat flower that could even be a clover leaf.

"The ring is too big for you, you won't wear it that much, let me have it."

"The girl who trusts her older sister will never have a man."

"You know that," my brother says and adds, laughing, that I shouldn't try to talk my sister into things.

My sister is different from me and my brother. My sister is almost ten years younger. My sister doesn't have dark locks. My sister is quiet and gets along well with everyone. My sister speaks softly and has a small nose. My sister loses her cell phone every four weeks, my bicycle twice a year, my clothes, my shoes, my watch, my hairpins. I never lose anything.

Once I lost my key, so I sat on the toilet; after reading the ingredients of the shower gel, the shampoo, the detergent, the deodorant, the soap package, phoning Anne, and counting the birthmarks on my upper arm and legs, I looked over at the washing machine; its door was open, so I lifted the gray rubber sealing ring, and there were the key and a few coins. But I looked in vain for the socks that had disappeared.

"Do you know the story about our written test?"

My sister shook her head. I listen to my brother.

"You weren't there," he said to my sister, "when she," he pointed at me, "tore up her learner's permit. Baba was waiting for us. At first, his face was full of expectation. When I said we had both failed the written exam for our drivers licenses, his face fell.

"'Don't worry, you can take the test again, no one passes the test on the first try. I myself had to do it over, and your mother, she didn't even try. She was so afraid of failing.'

"We couldn't contain our laughter any longer and yelled that we had passed.

"'Only idiots don't pass the test. I passed it with no mistakes, I'll teach you how to drive the right way,' Baba told us."

I take the sugar lying beside the coffee on the saucer and tear open the little packet with two pink cows on it with my teeth so that I can pour the contents into my palm. I dip my index finger, which I've just moistened with my tongue. I count twenty-eight sugar crystals on the tip of my finger before I dissolve them on my tongue.

"What else are you going to do today? Are you going to take a walk with Anne?" my brother asks me.

"You could go somewhere with her once in a while," I say to him.

"I'm fed up with having to justify everything I do. Leave me alone and stay out of my business. I know what I do, how often I do something with Anne—every day, if you must know. Like I say, I know what I have to do. I don't need you. Stop trying to micromanage everything I do. Otherwise I'm leaving."

"Go on, if you're going to threaten me with it. Well, get going," I say.

My sister is silent. I dip my finger a few times firmly in the sugar in the palm of my hand. My sister pokes my brother with her elbow, he pokes her, she pokes me, and I poke my brother.

"You won't get any more to stick if you keep dipping. You have to wet your finger really well, dip it once, roll it left and right, and put it in your mouth nice and easy."

My brother smiles and nudges me under the table.

He leaves, and we wish him well for his second written exam. Years have passed since the last time we were here. The sun is high in the midday sky, burns into my light skin. Shortly after my brother left, I drove to the Department of Motor Vehicles, got a plastic chair from the entry hallway, put it in front of the door, which kept opening and closing. My laptop is on my thighs, under it my skin sweats. I think of you, how you waited for us. A red Mercedes drives out of the parking lot past me onto the street, but I can't see who is at the wheel. My brother comes out and says he didn't pass the test.

"That's OK, you can take it again, no one passes the test on the first try. Even Baba had to take it again, and Anne, she didn't even try. She was so afraid of failing.

My brother laughs and yells, "No mistakes, and I was the first one finished."

"Only idiots don't pass the test. Baba passed it with no mistakes, too, unfortunately, I won't be able to teach you the right way to drive."

After we took the written exam the first time, we waited too long, and our learner's permits expired before we took the driving test.

The first thing Baba said to us when he picked us up at the airport on the sixteenth of October, 1991, was,

"In Switzerland, people take their dogs to bed with them."

It was the day my two-year-old sister was shot with a small pistol aimed at her ear. She screamed so loud that I had to hold my ears. After the screaming, two gold rings with sparkling gems adorned her little ear lobes. We were visiting Baba's cousin. Their home was nice, they had jobs, their daughter was very pretty, and they wore clothes that didn't come from charity.

We descended a long staircase into a basement. Baba liked going through stores, just looking. We couldn't buy anything. Sometimes Baba could afford a radio for one franc, an extension cord, boxes or devices that were broken. He wasn't allowed to work, so that gave him something to do. Anne hated the smell of old clothing, the dusty devices she hid in the attic until Baba found them and brought them back into the apartment. He tinkered with them for hours until they worked again. Then he put them back in the attic.

Baba's cousin got the idea, as long as we were all together, to make a video message to send to our relatives in Prizren. I shut myself in the bathroom and hoped I'd be forgotten. But my name was called at ever shorter intervals, I yelled that I had a stomach ache, my name was called at still shorter intervals until I had to come out, because they were not going to start without me. Anne's voice was unbearable. Repetition didn't bother her, everything was always repeated twenty times. She didn't yell, she didn't threaten, she repeated and repeated things until my brother and I were ready to do what she wanted. So I sat down on the edge of the patterned sofa, where Baba, Anne, and my brother were sitting, my sister in Baba's lap. Now we could send a message to everyone. As though we didn't already phone them more than enough.

Baba bought phone cards for foreign calls, then Anne and Baba shouted into the handset in the phone booth at the railroad station in Neuenegg. After Anne called my name for the twentieth time, I went into the booth and recited the sentences that she dictated:

"How are you? How is my cousin Zuhal, my cousin Ismail, their daughter Hürmet, the neighbors' daughter Gül, whom I always loved to play with, Mrki, the dog, how is the weather there? Here it's cold, very cold, everything is going very well at school, I'm in fourth grade, I'm a good student, I'll give you my brother now."

I left the booth, my brother went in and repeated the sentences that Anne said for him.

After a while I could not see anything in the booth, Baba was smoking in it, my brother waggled his hand in front of his face, and when he was allowed out, he was still holding his nose.

"Ask how Hatice is doing, what's her daughter doing, aren't they going to Vienna, is Bayram married yet, and would you ask whether Ayse has had her baby yet?"

Baba yelled into the handset, a cigarette between his lips, ashes on his sweater.

Anne asked if I wanted to go first.

"No," I said, and the camera pointed at me, a red light was blinking.

"Hello, you over there. Do you remember we called you yesterday?"

Anne whispered in my direction, "Ask how your cousin Zuhal and your cousin Ismail are doing."

I asked, "How is my cousin Zuhal and my cousin Ismail?"

Anne whispered in my direction, "How is the neighbor girl Gül doing, with whom you so loved to play."

I asked, "How is the neighbors' daughter Gül doing, with whom I always loved to play?"

Anne whispered in my direction, and I repeated after her, "How is Mrki, the dog, what's the weather like

102

there, here it's cold, very cold, everything is going very well at school, I'm in fourth grade, I'm a good student.

Then I waved awkwardly at the camera, which was still pointed at me, I kept waving and put on a smile until Baba asked why I was smiling like that and would I please stop waving.

I put my bicycle with the others in front of the Marzili outdoor pool and walk through the people lying on the ground.

Eli, that's the name of the woman I become acquainted with outside the restroom.

She talks and talks about her godmother, who died of diabetes recently and left her this ring, which she wears on her index finger and never takes off. It's become a little too small for her finger, because in recent weeks she's gained three and a half kilos.

Her godmother had the longest hair she'd ever seen on anyone.

"She was tall and slim, always wore this ring."

She shows it to me, raising her hand, the back of it toward me, and moves her outstretched finger slightly.

"When she was twenty-two, she went to Paris by herself; in the fifties, a Swiss woman didn't just up and do that. She knew that she would never return. As she was walking down the street, under the yellow street lights, humming a song, her hair moving with the wind, a light-blue Cadillac drove past her, put on the brakes, came backward, then kept up with her. At first, the man in the car whistled at her, then he started talking to her until she got into the car, married him, bore children for him, and allowed herself to be abused by him when she wanted to cut her hair and he was against it."

This aunt had a small apartment in rue d'Écureuil, where Eli sometimes goes now. The kitchen is too small for cooking because her aunt thought that women shouldn't have large kitchens so as not to be tempted to eat too much.

"She was in love with a man who didn't know anything about it, and she lived with a man whom she didn't love, from whom she could not get divorced, because she wanted to live in Paris no matter what, and look what she got, said her mother. The man she didn't love sucked everything out of her until she was completely emaciated and lay in her coffin on her long hair."

I'm the only one in a bathing suit. Eli talked me into going with her into the *Paradiesli*, the little paradise, the women's area. Beside us, two women sit opposite each other with their legs spread out having a conversation as though it were the most normal thing in the world to sit there naked and look each other in the eye.

All at once two naked old women jump up and start throwing pebbles.

"Get out, go, get lost!"

More and more naked women gather by the wall separating them from the rest of the outdoor pool. They are all yelling at once.

"Those bastards loosen bricks in the locker rooms and put little stones between them, those voyeurs. Beat it, you shameless sons of bitches."

I pull my bicycle from among all the others and ride from Marzili toward Bümpliz. I stop at a red light. In the car beside me I see a man singing to the music from the radio. His hand beats time on the steering wheel.

Green, I continue. The warm wind of summer caresses my face, makes my hair fly. The afternoon sun is low in the sky and makes me close my eyes. I still like one of the mansions in Schlösslistraße. Every time I ride by it, I admire the ivy-covered facade. Its two balconies are painted white and have flower pots. On one of the balconies there's a gray table between two white chairs, on the other a man is smoking a cigarette. The yard is spacious and divided by a gravel path. The branches of a cherry tree jut over the fence; as I ride by, I stick out my hand and grab for the soft, dark-red little balls. I stop at a red light, rid the cherries of the green leaves and twig. Two of them have worms, I drop them on the asphalt. I hold the bicycle firmly between my legs and rest my arms on the handle bars.

"Do you know which bus goes to the Inselspital, the Island Hospital?"

I point with my free hand to the bus station on the other side of the street. The light changes to green.

An island to which people travel to die. It's not a very pretty island, and it's not in the ocean. Trees grow only outside of it, flowers in pots. A great many insects fly around, a plague that no one will contain. They fly all year round, at all hours, and inject their poison into people. It's usually cold and very bright, which is why no animals other than insects can survive. With every breath you inhale the last breath of a person who has died. Every day new sick people arrive, just as every day dead people leave.

At the next red light I stay in the seat and prop myself up with one leg. I can feel the heat through my shoe.

A bit of blood runs down my calf. As soon as I look at it, it starts to burn. A horn sounds behind me, and I turn around, frightened. A woman is looking out through an open window.

"Green, it's green."

I try unsuccessfully to slip back into my shoe. The woman honks some more, I drag my bicycle to the side and watch her shake her head as she drives by me. The shoe has gotten warm. As I ride I spit the cherry stones onto the street.

I travel to Paris.

I enter the Montparnasse Cemetery with my head bowed. I say three kulhuvallahs and an elham for all the souls who rest there.

Leaves float down onto large and small gravestones. The dead leave behind them on the stones two numbers between which they lived, for people they never knew.

I use my fingers to calculate the ages of a few of them. I am the only one walking on the leaves between these stones of remembrance. The breeze is cool and warm at the same time, a leaf gets caught in my hair, I take it out, watch as it falls to the ground. The path is not visible. It's orange, red, and green. I take big strides to stir up as many leaves as possible. Sometimes I bump into a stone or something else. A walkway lined with chestnut trees that are all dying a little. The dead leaves lie down on the earth in which the dead lie. They will mingle, become earth, the leaf like the body.

Become earth.

We become the earth that our children and grand-children and their children will play with, in which they will plant flowers and trees, on which they will build the houses they will live in. They will walk on earth, get their hands dirty, smell it when it rains. At the ends of their lives they, too, will become earth, leaves will fall on them, mix with them.

The Montparnasse Cemetery is very well kept. The flowers growing from the earth above the coffins are fresh. There's a bridge that hovers low over the cemetery. Cars speed across it. People walk above the graves. Some throw paper or a plastic bottle without looking down. Others spit, trying to hit a gravestone.

"Do you know where the Montparnasse Cemetery is?" I asked a passerby as I was about to cross the bridge. She shook her head and kept going.

On my way out of the cemetery I say to the caretaker, "Auf Wiedersehen." Until we meet again.

Wind rustles the September leaves in the trees, they tremble till the leaves fall, are flattened under the soles of shoes, get blown away again and spread around the city.

Suddenly it's quiet. It rains. The sun peeks out again through the gray. The wind blows the leaves dry.

A woman stands in the sand with an open book. With the other hand she pushes a little girl in a swing, who makes no sound. The child presses her head against the rope to which she clings. Her hair covers half of her face. The only thing that moves are her legs, which dangle in the air in pink stockings and stir up the leaves on the ground.

Through sunglasses the world seems friendlier, a little warmer.

I sit down in the Café Odeon in the Old Town of Bern, where you liked to drink coffee. The whole room is empty, with mirrors on the walls. In the mirrors I see a hundred women in black dresses with sunglasses on their noses. They have their dark hair pulled back, their lips slightly parted. Their fingernails are lacquered red, a detail I notice only because they keep stroking their cheeks. They're wearing no jewelry. Once in a while they sip their colas. If I look at them, they all turn their heads toward me at the same time, and I look away. Aside from them, no one is there. Then I leave my half-empty glass and leave the empty room. My shoe gets stuck in a crack between the cobble stones, my bare foot stumbles on the wet ground. The cold of September first is quite palpable.

I go into Adrianos, a little sparrow flies in through the door, it flies under my table and pecks the remains of a nut roll, it keeps him busy for a long time.

A tall gentleman in a light suit comes toward me. He's wearing a straw hat. His white beard is neatly trimmed, when he laughs, his mustache covers his teeth, which look small, a bit discolored. He stands in front of me, the biography of Freud under his arm.

"Tell me, Miss, is the place beside you open?"

He reads his book while I look at him.

"Are you expecting someone?"

"No."

I take a deep breath. I try to store the fragrance of lemon aftershave so that I will always be able to recall it. Even long after the tall gentleman is gone, I walk past the tables and inhale, inhale till nothing is left to remind me of you. A year has passed.

"The ruling is negative. You can submit a new application after one year."

"What reason do you have? Please, I'd like to know the reason for this negative ruling. We all want to. So, what reason do you have?" I asked the assembled municipal councilors.

"We're not authorized to tell you the reason here and now. If you wish, you can ask for it in writing, you'll be informed in a few weeks. You have to leave the room now, we're expecting another family."

We were wearing our finest things, we had taken the whole day off and were all so excited that we had scarcely been able to sleep. On the way there, we quizzed each other about the history of Switzerland and laughed over the sentence, "I have integrated myself very well into Switzerland," which Anne repeated over and over. She repeated it so often that she left out letters or got words mixed up.

One year after we had submitted our application for Swiss passports, we were summoned to an interview in the municipal building in Neuenegg. We had now lived in Switzerland for almost twelve years and still could be deported.

Turkish became a foreign language, German our mother language, and with every Turkish word that disappeared from my mouth, Anne became more foreign to me, and Baba used ever more German words when he spoke to us.

Where were you born?

Why did you come to Switzerland?

Did you intend to take up residence in Switzerland from the beginning?

At what point did you start working?

Why do you want to become Swiss citizens?

Can you name our Federal Councilors?

How many cantons are there in Switzerland?

When was Switzerland founded?

Would you please spell Switzerland.

Do you belong to any Swiss association?[2]

No?

They wrote something on the notepads that lay on the table in front of them.

It took us years to get the required documents together. Doctors' statements, school transcripts, proof of employment, post-office account statements, bank-account statements, criminal records, debt-collection notices, birth certificates, the engagement notice, the marriage license, travel documents from the last few years.

On the way home, for the first time, no music played. Our neighbor from Macedonia was awaiting our arrival with camera in hand.

The moment before your picture is taken is terrifying.

The stiffening, the waiting, the silence.

Holding your breath and staring into a dark hole until it goes click.

[2]A Swiss association (*Verein*) is a legal structure in Swiss law, defined in the civil code. It is similar to the Anglo-American voluntary association. As the establishment of an association involves only little paperwork and no registration or fees, it is an important legal form in Switzerland and is often used by groups such as sport and social clubs for charitable or social purposes.

I don't like the German language; it's not my mother language. My mother doesn't speak German.

When I left the language of my childhood, I left my self.

I taught myself my mother language, I was ten.

After almost twenty years, my hands have become bigger; I feel the same as I did then.

I invented stories for my adult self. Stories that I thought up as if they were true. I wanted to be able to read those stories in the future and think back to a nice childhood. Whenever I wrote down what really happened, I tore the page out and threw it into the wastebasket.

After a while I believed the lies myself; I kept reading the stories until they became my past.

A single moment transports me from a past into a future that I'm afraid of.

I watch laughing people, on the street, on screens. I think of you, I think of your words, I think of your laugh. What is still to come? It doesn't stop today. I have not made up my mind to go on living, to live here. You are not here. Now I'm here. I live in Switzerland, where you have to consider yourself lucky to live.

In Switzerland, everyone is happy. Says my family in Prizren.

I was taken from my life. I was dropped into another life.

If my childhood had not been taken away, would I be more whole than the half I am today?

There, in my first life, I lived with Ismail, who now seems a stranger to me, who is going to have a child today, become a father. Ismail, with whom I played hide and seek all day, beside whom I slept. He exists only as I leave him. All at once Ismail is a man, and there's nothing in between. I do not understand the time in between. Every few years I come back for a moment to a former life where I no longer fit in because I've refit myself. Every time I've been there and come back, back to my present life, where I know my way around, where people who have lived their first lives here know me, I feel as though they are strangers.

No matter how long I'm here, you won't be here.

A father, a mother, three children can be seen. The youngest must have been about four years old, the boy between nine and twelve, the older girl, in a red dress, thirteen. They sit on a corner sofa that has a blue-gray pattern. The table in front of them is laden with food. There's a cake in the middle of it, which the youngest daughter is cutting into pieces with help from her mother. Loud music drowns out their words, sometimes you can make out something, but you have to listen very closely. The father, with a cigarette in his mouth, claps his hands in time to the music, the mother dances on the blue carpet with the younger daughter on her arm. They light a party bomb on the carpet, the boy puts a mask over his face and puts on a red nose, blows paper streamers into the smoke-filled air. On the wall it says "1996" in colored paper. The older girl sits still, then disappears suddenly when the family begins to count down from ten.

Four, three, two, one, I push the pause button on the Sony video recorder, its two vertical lines are no longer completely visible, then I leave the apartment in Bümpliz.

Downtown, crowds of people have gathered, shouting, laughing, throwing up. Couples embracing, children on their fathers' shoulders, older married couples with canes, sleeping children, drunks. A child beside me is holding onto the hem of my skirt. When I look down, the child starts to cry. It mistook me for its mother. The child cries, but it can't speak yet, first it must forget everything that there was before it came into the world, so that it can't betray the secret to anyone. Just as we tell the dead that they are dead and have no more business in this world, we help children to forget and give them freedom.

The parents come, snatch it away.

The child looks at me as the mother gives it pet names. Rockets shoot into the sky, the smell of cigarettes and alcohol hangs in the air.

I push through the mass of people. A rose seller stops me, asks if I would buy a rose, I nod, I have no money with me.

Ten, nine, the big bell tolls, the gray tower is brightly lit, disappears into the mist.

Eight, seven, six, five, the gold of the last judgment shines above the entrance of the cathedral, the fire, the burning people, the children, the monsters, the angels.

Three, two, another child cries out, pulls his father's hair, who looks about impatiently for the mother, who rushes up with two glasses of champagne.

One.

The picture stands still, flickers. For fear of becoming petrified I do not stand still, I walk through the crowd of petrified people. I hear myself breathing. The sky is black, the stars barely visible. High above, an old married couple stands at an open window. I hadn't noticed them before. The woman is leaning out the window. The husband is holding the curtain back so that he can see the crowd. My purse falls to the ground, I bend down. The legs of the crowd are like a dark forest with trees that didn't grow tall enough.

The pause feels a little longer this year. What has happened since the last standstill? I cannot remember. I've breathed a few times, uttered a few sounds, looked, I think.

My heavy body is suddenly light as a word.

Once again we had bought too much. Party bombs, colorful balloons, sweets, salty things.

I had put on a red dress. My brother and sister helped me decorate the white wall with colorful paper. We did that every year, and every year loud music blared from the TV. On top of the TV stood the running camera.

The cake that Anne had baked, as she did every New Year's Eve, tasted good, I liked it even more the next morning with a glass of cold milk.

We sat on the corner sofa with the gray-blue pattern. Baba clapped in time to the music with the cigarette in his mouth. I waited for the stillness, for the moment when everyone stiffened. The fear mounted with every number of the countdown. The uneasy feeling before the stillness gripped me again, I could hardly breathe, felt very light, got up abruptly and shut myself in my room. Now, it must be at this exact moment, the stiffening.

Once upon a time, never upon a time.

Einwandern, auswandern . . .

© Matthias Günter

About the Author

Meral Kureyshi was born in 1983 in Prizren in the former Yugoslavia, where her family belonged to the Turkish-speaking minority. She immigrated to Switzerland with her family in 1992 and now lives in Bern. She has studied German literature at the Swiss Literature Institute in Biel, founded a poetry workshop for children, and now works as a freelance writer. Her first novel, *Elephants in Our Yard*, was nominated for the Swiss Book Prize in 2015, won several awards, and has been translated into many languages. Her second novel, *Fünf Jahreszeiten*, was published in 2020, and was awarded «Das zweite Buch» prize by the Marianne and Curt Dienemann Foundation.

About the Translator

Bob Cantrick grew up in the United States and attended the University of Rochester, NY, and the Johannes Gutenberg University in Mainz, earning a BA degree in German. He did graduate work at the universities of Cologne and Bonn on a fellowship, then continued studies in Germanic languages and literature at Indiana University (Bloomington) on a teaching assistantship. Among many other things, he worked as a freelance translator, in-house translator and editor, and legal secretary-translator. In recent years he concentrated on literary translation. In 2016 he was one of the winners of the New Books in German Translation Competition, and in 2017 he won second prize in the John Dryden Translation Competition for his translation of the first part of *Mario and the Magician* by Thomas Mann, published in the June 2018 issue of *Contemporary Critical Studies*. In 2018 he was one of the featured translators at the Festival Neue Literatur in New York City. He also translated *The Pope's Left Hand* by Friedrich Christian Delius, which was published by Noumena Press in 2019. He died in November 2020.

Sadly, Robert Cantrick did not live to see the publication of his translation from German of Meral Kureyshi's *Elephants in Our Yard*. He died on November 4, 2020, due to the effects of throat cancer treatment.

It was at high school in Alabama that Bob discovered his interest and aptitude for the German language. In 1961, when he was 17, he had the opportunity to go to Germany to participate in a youth work camp for the summer. It was to be the first of several trips there to study, work, and absorb the German language and culture.

Bob practiced many trades during his work life, including the translation of documents for the books that make up *The Communist International in Lenin's Time* series. It was only after retiring that he turned his hand to literary translation. In the relatively short period he devoted to this new trade, his translations earned him recognition from both the New Books in German and the John Dryden Translation Competitions.

When Bob undertook something, he did not do it in half measures. He poured his considerable translation, creative writing and life skills into faithfully and sensitively conveying in English what and how the author wrote in German.

If he had been able to write this afterword himself, he undoubtedly would have wanted to acknowledge the generous collaboration of Heidi Heigel, who reviewed the complete translation of *Elephants in Our Yard*. He would also have wished to recognize "the anonymous denizens of the LEO online dictionary and forum, too numerous to credit individually, for their wise and perceptive insights into the intricacies of the German language," as he wrote in his previously published translation, *The Pope's Left Hand* by Friedrich Christian Delius. And finally, he would have wanted to thank R.J. Allinson and Rachel Thern of Noumena Press for all their hard work in producing this book.